FIRE AND TEARS SERIES

Brightarrow Burning
Darkness Singed
Dawn Ignited

Fire and Tears: Series Collection Books 1-3

DARKNESS SINGED

FIRE AND TEARS
BOOK TWO

ISABO KELLY

T&D PUBLISHING

DARKNESS SINGED

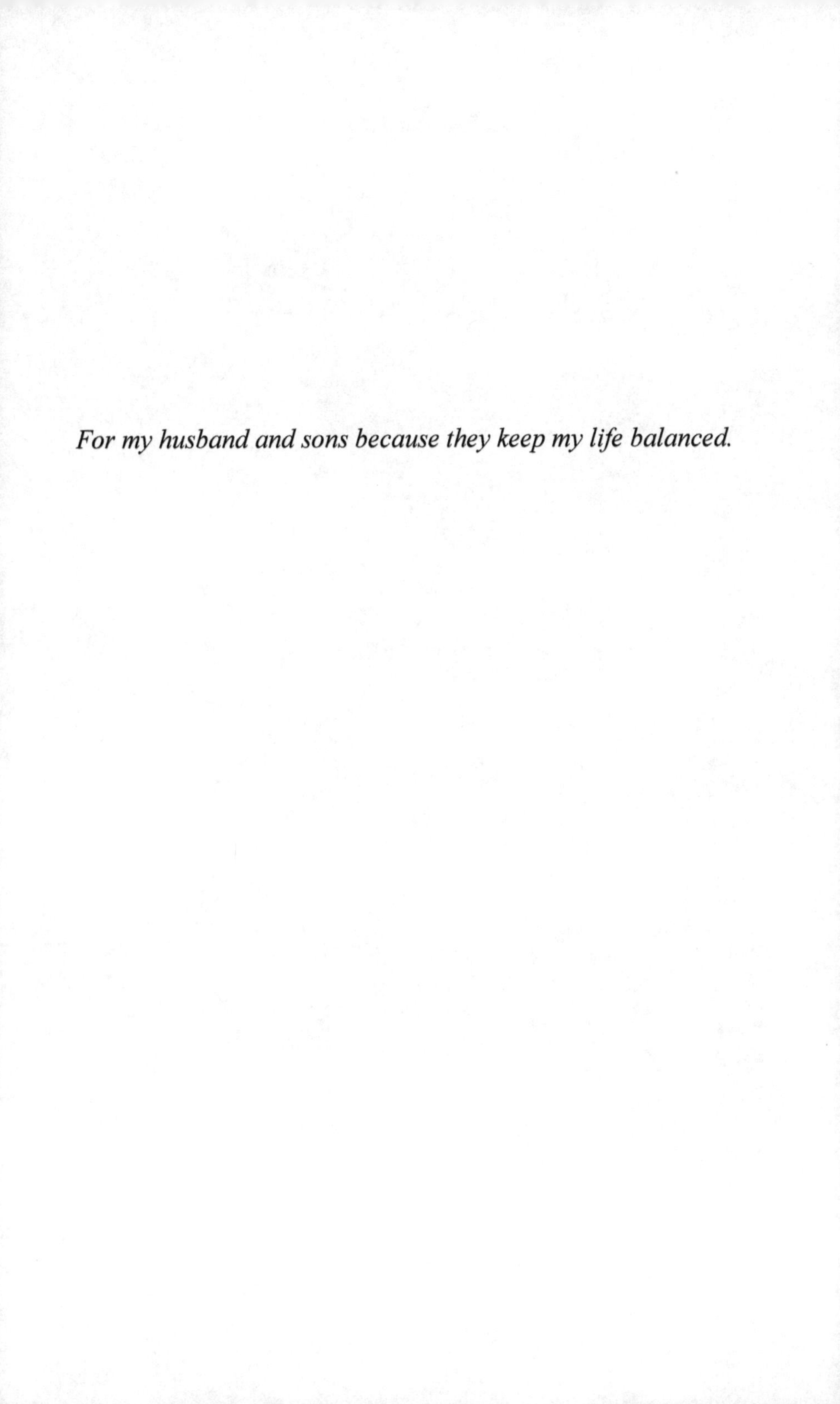

For my husband and sons because they keep my life balanced.

CHAPTER ONE

Nuala of Glengowyn kept her gaze forward and her shoulders proud but loose, determined to hide the tension twisting her stomach from the soldiers surrounding her. She hadn't been outside Glengowyn in nearly a century, most certainly hadn't been allowed to leave since the war between the Sorcerers and the humans of Sinnale began. This trip, necessary though it was, would not have been her choice for her first excursion back into Sinnale.

She rode near the center of the military escort—both human and elven—her bow and quiver bumping gently against her back, comforting in their familiarity. The less comfortable knives in the scabbards strapped to her waist were a steady reminder of the danger. Even the glowering, deadly elf riding beside her couldn't calm her anxiety.

But she'd be damned if she let Einar see her fear.

Lifting her chin to steady herself, she studied the grassy plains bracketing the road from Glengowyn to Sinnale. They'd left the safety of the forest not long ago, and she'd felt exposed and vulnerable ever since. The human city was in view, less than half a mile away, the buildings and houses rising and falling like a clunky, awkward mountain range against the deep blue sky. Beyond and to the west of the city, the real mountains of the Arei-atun Range rose up like purple and gray sentinels. The contrast between nature and the manmade structures was stark and sobering.

"You're hiding your tension well, my lady," the towering man beside her said quietly, for her ears only. "But your mare is beginning to react to your anxiety."

Nuala scowled at Einar then focused on her mount for several moments, working at relaxing her body, her grip on the reins, her knees against the horse's sides. She felt the large gray relax as well and only then realized how tightly the mare had been holding herself. If not for Einar's comment, the gray would have started fidgeting openly soon, revealing just how scared her rider was. The fact that Einar had noticed Nuala's unease so easily robbed any feelings of gratitude she might have had for his discreet help, though.

But she was nothing if not well trained to be polite. "Thank you. I will make an effort to control my reactions better."

"You have always been in full control of your reactions, my lady. To everything."

He didn't look at her as he spoke, his gaze sweeping their surroundings, ever watchful. But she heard the bite in the comment, the subtle jab most wouldn't have noticed. She refused to respond, not entirely sure she could censor herself in that moment. Not when she expected a physical attack with every breath. And most definitely not with *him*.

She kept her own gaze on the high grass beside the road

so she wouldn't have to face Einar and risk him seeing her inner turmoil. He was the only man, the only person, who had ever been able to read her with any level of accuracy. Even her cousins, Ulric and Althir, who'd looked after her after her parents were killed in the first goblin war, could never read her moods or thoughts.

Einar was an entirely different story.

She acknowledged, reluctantly, that the danger posed by the Sorcerers and the war weren't the only reasons for her anxiety. When the Darkness of Glengowyn, personal bodyguard to the elf king and queen, had been assigned as her bodyguard, Nuala very nearly backed out.

But to do so would have revealed too much. To everyone. Including *him*.

"You will reach the city safely," Einar murmured. "I swear it."

She continued to stare at the grass so he wouldn't see her expression, though she was sure he wasn't looking at her as he spoke. His words made her throat squeeze tight. "I know you'll do what you can," she returned quietly. "But no caravan reaches Sinnale without being attacked. This will be no different."

"I'm not afraid of the Sorcerers' minions."

"Of course *you're* not." As soon as she spoke, she wished she could take it back. Too much. Those few words revealed too much. And Einar would know. He would understand everything if she wasn't very careful.

She thought maybe he understood too well already.

"You've no need to fear them either."

"I'm not the warrior here. I make the weapons. I don't go into battle with them."

"And I have no intention of risking you in battle now."

A traitorous part of her heart lifted at that. "When the minions attack, you'll have no choice."

He actually turned to look at her and because she could feel his stare on the side of her face, she met his gaze. Black as the deepest, moonless night.

"You think I will let those abominations near you? I have sworn to protect you as I would the king and queen. You doubt me?"

She realized he was actually offended. Most wouldn't have seen it. He hid his emotions better even than she did. Most of the elves of Glengowyn thought he didn't have any. But she'd always seen beyond his façade. The sword cut both ways between them.

"I don't doubt your ability to protect me, Einar. But if the traitors have told the Sorcerers about me, they'll be waiting for this particular caravan. You may not have the choice to keep me out of the fight."

"You're not trained for combat. Do not engage the enemy. Stay beside me, and I will see you safe."

She shook her head and looked away. He was the most deadly elf in all of Glengowyn. But he wasn't invincible. No matter what the others thought.

The one thing in her favor was that, outside of the traitor elves, no one from Sinnale had seen her in the last two human generations. None of the minions would recognize her—if they still retained any memories of their human lives after the Sorcerers were done with them. And she doubted any of the traitors would dirty their hands in an actual caravan attack. The Sorcerers never left the city, and none of them would know her on sight anyway.

The attack, *when* it came, would likely be no different from any other. The heavy guard surrounding her and the wagons of her arrows, both her normal enchanted arrows and the special weapons the Sinnale were only now being allowed to trade for, should have no trouble repelling the minions.

But as she studied the long, waving sheets of golden-green grass along the roadside, a chill skittered along her shoulders and her mare danced a step or two beneath her before she reined her in. Nuala's stomach tightened.

She hadn't been allowed to take risks of any kind since the end of the second goblin war, not since she'd developed the weapon she was now delivering to Sinnale, the weapon that had helped the elves win that war. Once the conflict was over, her particular magic, and her skill in wielding it, had been considered too valuable to endanger.

The sudden rake of terror along her spine could have had something to do with her lack of recent experience with tension and fear. Nothing in the grass signaled a change. The city's outlier buildings grew closer with each clomp of the horses' hooves, close enough now she could see some of the damage to the structures at the edge of Noman's Land, not far from where they would enter the city.

Still, she couldn't shake the sensation of being watched.

A quick glance at Einar, then the other warriors, assured her they were keeping their focus on the surroundings. No one paid her any particular attention. Not for lack of curiosity, she was sure, but because the Darkness of Glengowyn had ordered them to ignore her. Staring would not only distract them from the possible dangers, it would single her out as someone significant. The soldiers were following that order perfectly. She was outwardly no different from any other mounted elf in the caravan.

She studied the grass again, frowning in concentration as she searched the shifting waves.

That focus saved her life.

CHAPTER TWO

An arrow flashed silver in the glinting sunshine, so fast and true, Nuala might have been impressed if not for the fact that the arrow was heading for her. She spurred her mare forward, ducking low to the gray's neck, and still felt the arrow whisper just above her spine. She screamed a warning at the same instant, praying to the Goddess that Einar wasn't hit by the deadly missile meant for her. She'd never survive that.

Almost before she felt the weapon whistle past, more missiles flew into their ranks. And a moment later, a horde of minions rose from the grass, swords high, silent as the wind as they attacked.

Then Einar raced up beside her, shouting, "Ride! To the city."

She didn't pause to think, just spurred the gray forward. Fortunately, the animal was war trained and didn't panic. She charged over the rutted road, closing in on safety, without any reaction to the sounds of clashing metal and the cries of the wounded and dying.

Keeping her head low, Nuala glanced over her shoulder, confirming Einar kept pace with her. They moved so fast through the middle of their own people, the minions had no chance to reach them—another part of Einar's plan. But the column of protection wouldn't take them all the way to Sinnale. Too soon, they raced beyond the fighting soldiers and into the open to cover the remaining three hundred yards.

The appearance of three minions in their path startled her enough she screamed. Einar changed directions, forcing her and her mare parallel to the city without slowing their run. Behind her, she heard a shout, and another glance back confirmed a dozen minions followed.

"Where did they come from?" she yelled.

"Later." Einar searched the edge of the city. "We need the cover of the buildings." He angled his horse back toward Sinnale, and she followed his lead.

This time when something blocked their path neither reacted fast enough to change directions. Her gray reared. Nuala tightened her thighs, keeping her seat, but the stench of death emanating from the Sorcerer made her gag. Her mare danced under her, faced with a horror beyond her training. Einar pulled his sword and pushed his own mount in front of Nuala's to guard her from the new threat.

The Sorcerer smiled, glanced beyond them. And vanished.

In his place, three of the traitor elves closed in.

Nuala had no time to absorb the shock of this new development. The minions following them were too close. Einar could handle the elves. She shifted her mount to face their rear, dropped the reins, and slid her bow over her head. The gray knew what to do in battle, and Nuala could guide her with her legs, leaving her hands free to use her weapon. She covered Einar's back, firing arrow after arrow as the minions came within range. Of the dozen, eight fell with mortal or near-mortal wounds. Two more were injured enough to slow them down. Only two made it through her barrage.

She tried to keep her mount, using the strong wood of her weapon to bat at the minions while her horse reared and thrashed. The mare held the two attackers off, but when the wounded minions joined the fight, Nuala knew she and the mare were outnumbered. Her greatest fear in that moment was that the minions would get around her and get to Einar.

She had two arrows left in her quiver, but at close range, the weapon was less useful. As her horse whipped around sharply and kicked at one of the attackers, Nuala grabbed the mare's mane in one hand for balance and dropped the bow over her head, across her back. She reached for the reins, but they'd slipped beyond easy grasp and she overbalanced trying to get them. When her gray spun and jumped sideways at the same time to avoid the swing of a sword, Nuala's stomach clenched as she was tossed to the ground.

She hit hard on her left side, the jolt knocking the wind from her. Over the sounds of clashing metal and screaming horses, she heard Einar call her name. Three of the human slaves stalked toward her as the fourth turned toward Einar and the traitors trying to subdue him. With a wheezing gasp, she stumbled to her feet, barely able to suck in a breath.

Her left arm hurt but didn't feel broken. And when she drew both knives from their scabbards at her waist, her left hand worked enough to hold the hilt firmly. She wasn't a trained warrior, hadn't been allowed to train, but that hadn't stopped her from learning a few things over the years. Thanks to Ulric and Althir's secret lessons.

She waited and watched the three minions as they approached. One smiled at her. The others remained strangely passive, as if the fight wasn't something happening to them at all. One of the expressionless men limped badly, and she realized her gray had got in a clean kick, damaging his leg. He dragged the wounded limb, seemingly unaware of the injury.

Nuala swallowed and raised her knives.

"Stop." A deep voice rose up behind the three attackers.

A familiar voice. But not the one she'd hoped to hear.

One of the traitors passed between the minions, his smirk both smug and confident. "I'll handle the weapons master. Help the others with her guard."

She didn't dare take her eyes off the traitor as he neared, even to check on Einar. The fact that the others were being sent to the fight against him meant he was alive. She could hear the sounds of swords clashing, the screams of pain that weren't Einar's. Even three more minions wouldn't be enough.

"He'll kill them all, Byral," she said as the traitor approached. "You know he will."

"But elves can't kill other elves." Byral stalked her, his gait smooth and graceful. Blood splattered his dark gray tunic. But he didn't look injured.

To kill another elf was a taboo among her kind, so ingrained in their society most elves believed it was physically impossible for one elf to kill another.

Only recently had she been made aware of the truth. But this traitor didn't need to know that. "The minions will be slaughtered. Einar will disable the other two traitors."

Byral's eyes shifted slightly, their deep, intense blue clouding just a little. "Surprising," he said with a slight tilt of his head. "I didn't think the Darkness ever left the king's and queen's sides. But..." He shrugged. "I suppose for you, they would take the risk."

"Why?"

She didn't have to elaborate. Byral knew what she was asking. Rather than answer, he angled around her, circling, looking for an opening in her weak defenses.

"They won't harm you," he said. "The Sorcerers. They can offer you a lot."

"I'm no traitor." He was close enough that the stench of death magic corrupting him filled her nostrils. "They've been teaching you?" She was surprised by that. The Sorcerers were jealous of their powers, despite what they'd told the traitors. She'd been led to believe they hadn't shared any of their magic with the elves.

"Only me." His smirk returned. "I promised them you in return."

Nuala's stomach clenched and her heartbeat jumped. She didn't show the reaction outwardly but fear clogged her throat. Only an act of will kept her from panting as panic crept in around her control. "I won't go quietly. And you can't kill me."

"But I can wound you enough to make you cooperate."

Rather than respond, she focused on her grip on the two knives, making sure she was prepared. When Byral lunged suddenly and with a speed she hadn't anticipated, she reacted without thought. One wide step shifted her out of his reach and gave her an opening to slide her knife across his biceps. He snarled and whipped back to face her, diving into another attack before she had time to feel satisfied with her strike.

This time, she stumbled and fumbled, swinging her knives awkwardly as she tried to put space between them. He didn't raise his sword except to bat away her flailing weapons. He wanted her alive, even if he knew he could kill her—knowledge she wasn't sure he possessed.

She tripped over the grass tangling around her boots and dropped to one knee, losing a knife in the barely controlled fall. Byral chuckled. Behind him, Einar roared her name again. The fact that he was alive dampened her fear. She held Byral's gaze as he loomed over her. With a sniff of disgust, he grabbed her arm and jerked her to her feet.

"They shouldn't have allowed you out of Glengowyn. But I profit from their mistake."

"No."

She saw the slight flicker in his eyes, the beginnings of suspicion, the instant before she plunged her knife into his heart, burying the weapon to the hilt. His blue eyes widened, his mouth dropped open and his grasp on her arm fell away. He looked at the knife in his chest then met her gaze, his mouth moving in a silent denial.

"You should have known better," she murmured. "The *Or'roan* takes you now. Forever death."

The *Or'roan*, a curse only the king and queen could inflict on the elves, ended their existence forever—no afterlife, no rebirth into future lives, no hope for any future existence. The end of all they'd ever been and all they would be was greatly feared by every elf. And all but one of the traitors was currently under the *Or'roan.*

Terror transformed Byral's once starkly handsome face into a distorted mask. "No," he forced out with his last breath. He never lost the grip on his sword, even when he collapsed.

She swallowed down the bile in her throat, retrieved the knife she'd lost in the grass when she'd tripped, and forced herself to focus on Einar and his fight. She would deal with the fact that she'd just done the unthinkable, the impossible, later.

The minions hadn't stood a chance against the Darkness. They lay in silent heaps around the swirling rage that was Einar in battle. The two remaining elves were both bloodied and retreating under the hail of Einar's attack. The flow of the fight moved them closer to the city, and Nuala realized suddenly that the elves' retreat was strategic. She didn't dare call out to warn Einar for fear of distracting him. But she knew with certainty the traitors were drawing him into a trap.

The Sorcerer.

She scanned the area, noting with an ache that would hurt more when she had time that Einar's horse was among the wounded, its dark sides no longer rising and falling. Her mare was nowhere in sight, and she could only assume the animal had been smart enough to flee. Most of the Glengowyn steeds would fight to the death. But Nuala couldn't face the thought of another life lost so was glad the animal's training had failed.

She worked her way toward Einar, watching carefully to make sure the traitors didn't notice her. But the Darkness was no ordinary elf and the traitors didn't dare look away. In the distance, she could hear the sounds of battle from the caravan.

She and Einar had gone too far east for her to find help from that direction, though. The edge of the city was near enough for them to reach at a sprint, but she had no idea what dangers lurked in those streets. And the forest was too far away for them to make a run for it on foot.

Somewhere out there, the Sorcerer who'd stopped their escape was waiting. She couldn't see or sense him. But she knew he was there. Somewhere.

She got close enough to Einar to guard his back even as the traitors continued to lure them closer to the city's outer buildings. The two elves spread out, forcing Einar to face one or the other, an attempt to outflank him.

Refusing to think about her actions, Nuala flipped the knife so she held the tip in her fingers. With a flick of her wrist, she sent her last weapon flying. It struck the traitor on Einar's left, burying deep into the space between his shoulder and chest. Not a deadly hit. Her aim wasn't that good. But the injury was enough to make him drop his sword.

He looked at the knife with the same dumbfounded shock as Byral had, facing her with wide eyes an instant before Einar drove a sword through his throat.

The final elf shouted something she didn't catch and fled toward the city. She reached out to take Einar's arm, afraid he'd try to follow the retreating man, but Einar stood solid and immovable, the blood on his sword dripping into the soil. The stench of death and blood clogged her throat, bringing back memories long buried.

"We need cover," Einar said as he glanced toward the caravan fight, then back at the city. "Forest is too far."

Prickles of tension raced along her arms. "The Sorcerer is there." She nodded at the city even as she continued to scan their surroundings. They stood out in the open, horribly exposed and vulnerable. With each breath, she anticipated another attack.

"He's not," Einar stated.

Not bothering to explain, he grabbed her hand and raced toward the dubious cover of the outlier buildings.

CHAPTER THREE

The transition from rough grass to cobbled streets jolted through Nuala's calves as they barreled between two scarred brick structures and into the city proper. When they weren't followed, when no magical attack came, she actually felt relief wash through her.

But when she would have slowed to a trot, Einar tightened his hold on her hand and continued to pull her along at a fast run. He turned corners, raced down alleys and small streets, hurried along the edge of open courtyards, keeping her close to the looming shadows of the surrounding buildings as they went.

After so long, she barely recognized the city. Empty, quiet, the stench of things she remembered from another war permeating the air. The bright sun seemed somehow diminished, cooled and weakened by the pervasive gloom that hung over the streets.

Einar finally slowed to a trot and then a fast walk.

"Where are we?" she asked, her heart thumping from both the run and her own fear.

"Noman's Land."

"What happened to the Sorcerer? Why didn't he attack?"

"He was never real."

She frowned, wanting to ask more questions, but Einar didn't give her a chance.

"We need to get inside."

"Why don't we just head toward Sinnale-held territory?"

"We need time. And a plan." He pushed her back against a brick façade and held her in place for several long moments.

She listened intently, waiting for…something. The area was eerily silent, only the faint creak of wood and the barest brush of moving air. No rustling leaves. No bird song. No quiet hum of the forest. Nuala had never felt so disconnected and displaced.

Einar remained motionless for what seemed like a very long time. Then he ushered her across the empty street and straight into a relatively intact building. The small, three-story structure had most of its windows and shutters in place, and the front door was solid, if unlocked.

"Is this safe?" she said, so quietly human ears would never detect the sound.

"Abandoned."

When he pushed her into the cool darkness, Nuala took a moment to let her eyes adjust and her heart rate slow.

"Are you hurt?" Einar asked from his position near the door. He was studying the street, not looking at her.

That lack of attention was as much of a relief as the relative safety of being inside. "No," she said to keep him from facing her for a few more moments. "Are you?"

He didn't answer. She swept his big body with a searching gaze, frowning as she looked for wounds. There was a superficial cut on his left biceps, visible through his ripped shirt sleeve, and a tear in his leather trousers, just across the thick muscle of his thigh. But she couldn't see anything that looked serious.

Satisfied, she turned in a small circle to survey their hiding spot.

They stood in what had been the foyer to a smart, elegant townhouse. Not that the elegance remained. But at one time, she was sure someone of wealth and significance had called this place home. The walls were hung with faded, dirty silk that might have been a pale color sometime in its past. No furniture remained, but stairs to the left led to the upper floors and several closed doors flanked the open entryway. Spaces that had probably contained pictures or mirrors or some other decoration left lighter rectangles in the grime covering the silk wall drapings. The floor was bare wood but inlaid in a beautiful pattern, which would look stunning after a clean and polish.

An ache of loss settled around her chest. Had the owners of this once-beautiful home been killed? Sacrificed to the Sorcerers' spells? Turned minion? Did a human live who might one day reclaim this place?

Caught up in her sense of sorrow, she jumped when she felt Einar's hand on her shoulder. Without turning to face him, she said, "I hate war. I always have."

"I know."

His understanding only made her throat tighten further.

"We can rest here." Einar's deep voice was quiet in the

stillness. "But not for long. This is too close to the Sorcerers' territory."

"We're that far east?"

"We entered the city in their territory."

She blinked. She hadn't realized. "How did you know where to go? Are you sure we're outside their borders?"

The Sorcerers' borders were guarded with deadly, nasty spells. They'd been lucky not to trigger any. Or else Einar had talents he'd never revealed to her.

"We're safe for now. I'm certain we're in Noman's Land."

She released a pent-up breath. "And after we've rested?" She finally found the courage to face him. They didn't have time for her to fall apart. Not yet.

"Then we make our way to the Sinnale. And hope they don't kill us on sight."

"Why would they?"

He dropped his chin to meet her gaze. "Unknown elves crossing over from Noman's Land? Only traitor elves should be coming from this direction."

"But someone in the caravan must have made the city limits. They'll tell the humans what's happened."

Einar didn't look convinced. "If they realize we survived the attack. But there are very, very few in this city who will recognize me. And no human will know you on sight, even those who survived the caravan attack."

The king had put a small glamour spell on her, just enough to keep humans from remembering her too well once she was no longer in their company—a precaution that now seemed more of a hindrance.

"We can't assume a friendly reception," Einar finished.

"Should we try to return to Glengowyn? When the sun sets?"

His frown deepened. "One traitor survived the attack. He'll tell the Sorcerers we're alive and in the city. They'll assume we'll try to either return to Glengowyn or make the Sinnale border tonight."

"You think they'll attempt to take us again?"

He met her gaze. "They will come for you again. Yes."

She didn't miss his pointed omission. "You think they'll kill you?"

"They'll try."

The very thought of Einar being killed left a hollow ache in the pit of her stomach. She might not admit to him how she felt, but her feelings for the Darkness of Glengowyn had remained constant for more than two hundred years. Even though she couldn't have him for her own, she'd had the comfort of knowing he was on this plane, nearby, close enough to see and touch, smell and hear. He'd been a part of her life for as long as she could remember. He'd been her heart's desire for so long now she couldn't even begin to image her world without him in it.

To fight back the devastation even the thought of his death brought her, she lifted her chin and said, "You're no easy kill, Darkness. They'll be cautious."

"But you're valuable enough to risk my wrath."

Her heart tripped a little when he said "my" and not "the wrath of Glengowyn". But she realized he hadn't meant the comment as anything personal. He protected her because the king and queen asked it of him. Nothing more.

"What do you suggest?" She had to keep her focus on the

situation. To think too much about Einar robbed her of her sense and reason.

"We keep cover here for the night. I'll attempt to get a message to the Sinnale. And the king. You'll be safer if they know to expect us. They may even be able to send aid."

"You don't think the minions will be sent to hunt us down here?"

"Both sides patrol Noman's Land. We'll be in danger from humans and minions."

"That's not really an answer to my question."

He held her gaze without blinking as he said, "They'll hunt for us here."

"We have allies in the Sinnale. I still think we should work our way toward their border."

"Not until I know our way will be safe. You're too valuable."

She snorted at his last statement and spun away. Goddess, how she hated being reminded every day, every hour of just how *valuable* she was to everyone else. Everyone but him.

She forced back that thought. It wasn't fair to him. But a thread of bitterness crept into her voice when she said, "And how will you ensure I'm protected now?"

There was no emotion in his tone when he answered. "The owls."

She nodded in understanding. He had a special affinity with the owls that carried messages for the elves. They did so only because Einar asked. The birds weren't trained carriers, not the way such creatures might have been trained in the past. Owls assisted the Glengowyn elves because Einar requested their assistance. The clever beings wouldn't continue in that job if Einar died. Something most elves had probably forgotten.

Like they'd forgotten elves were physically capable of killing other elves.

That thought reminded her vividly of the life she'd taken. She suspected Einar had killed other elves before—though most would have been unaware of the acts—but she'd been subject to the taboo her entire life. She could hardly believe she'd really done it, that she'd been able to.

That she didn't regret the act as she'd assumed she would.

Those thoughts led her down a path she didn't have time for. "So," she said, facing him. "We wait here for a short time? Or for the night? Will you request an owl come here?"

He stared at the floor, his brow furrowed. "I don't like to ask them to come to Noman's Land. But we have no choice."

"We can move closer to the edge of the city, so they won't have to fly too far into danger."

"The Sorcerers will be watching the city border closest, assuming I'll try to return you to Glengowyn."

"You're sure?"

"It's what I would tell them if I were one of the traitors. It's what most would do in this situation, given your value. So we'll stay here for a few hours, watch to see if we've been found. Once it's full dark, we'll find a new location."

"Toward the Sinnale?"

He dipped his chin in a sharp affirmative. "I'll have an owl come to me in our next location, if it's safe."

She stared at him for a few more minutes, caught by his intensity. To escape, she glanced down at his injured arm. "I can wrap that for you." She gestured to the wound.

He gave it a cursory glance. "It's only a scratch."

"But neither of us can afford to have you weakened." She spun in a slow circle, then started opening doors. When she found a room that contained a couch, she led him inside. "Sit," she ordered.

Without supplies, her only option for binding the wound was the hem of her riding robe. "Your knife." She held out a hand without looking at him and pulled up the long length of material.

"It's not necessary."

"Don't argue." She wiggled her fingers, still focused on the material in her hand. His presence threw her off balance and looking directly at him made it worse. They hadn't spent this much time together, alone and in close proximity, since…

She didn't want to think about the last time.

After the knife hilt settled gently into her palm, she sliced a few lengths of silk along the split front hem of the robe. It would leave a wider V in the front, but since they had to travel quickly, she was considering cutting off the length completely anyway. Once the sun set, the early autumn nights were too cold to get rid of the over-robe altogether. And it was designed to allow easy, free movement, with slits in front and back so she could sit astride her horse without the long material getting in the way. It had stayed out of her way during the earlier fight too. But those lengths of material could be put to better use. And the less she had to worry about right now, the better.

Once she had sufficient improvised bandages, she turned to Einar. "Take your tunic off," she said, her voice as firm and emotionless as she could make it.

She tried not to be affected as he stood, removed his scabbard belt, then slipped his short vest off and dragged his tunic up over his head. Unfortunately, she couldn't hold back her quickly drawn breath when the magnificent musculature of his chest was revealed in full.

This wasn't the first time she'd seen him bare-chested, but the sight never ceased to stir her. When she looked up, she found him staring at her, his dark eyes nearly black in the dim light leaking in through grimy windows. She swallowed and focused on his arm. Her heartbeat sped as she drew near enough to feel the heat of his skin and smell the tangy combination of his natural spicy musk mixed with the sweat of battle. With Einar, that combination had always overwhelmed her better judgment, targeting her most desperate desires. Only with him.

Yet another reason she'd spent so many years avoiding him.

Though her pulse pounded in her ears, she concentrated on making her hands steady, her touch gentle. She used one length of material to gently blot the worst of the blood away. Some still seeped slowly from the injury, but not enough to be dangerous. Once she'd gotten the area as clean as possible with a dry cloth, she used another length to tightly bind the wound.

His muscles flexed under her touch, which didn't help. "Relax," she ordered, her voice irritatingly husky.

He let out a long, slow exhale that brushed over the top of her head, and his biceps relaxed. She noticed at a glance, however, that his stomach muscles were tightly clenched. When she risked a peek at his face, his jaw was also tight, and he stared at the wall across from where they stood.

She turned back to her work, knowing she shouldn't have risked this kind of proximity for this long. Einar had more power over her body and heart than any other elf. A fact they were both growing more aware of with each passing moment.

When she'd tied off the bandage, satisfied it would do for now, she stepped back and gestured at his leg without actually looking down. "Are you cut or was it just your trousers?"

"It's nothing."

"Nothing as in no blood, or nothing as in you don't wish me to bandage the wound?"

His gaze jumped from the wall to her and she took another involuntary step back. Heat, promise, need and something she didn't want to admit seeing blazed out at her, an arrow right into her heart.

"You made it clear," he said quietly, "that your magic was not something you could sacrifice. We should not remain this close. And I should *not* take off any more clothing around you."

Her throat was too dry to even swallow. She could feel it, as she was certain he could—the *Shaerta*. Humans called it elf-fire. And sometimes elf-tears because it was addictive to them. Between elves, it was strong but didn't cause permanent damage with exposure. What *would* happen if they heeded its call, if they allowed themselves to truly bond, was a melding of their magics. The results were unpredictable. She wouldn't know until it was too late what form her abilities would take after a bonding.

Queen Rohannah had made it very clear that Nuala's talents were too valuable to risk.

"You agreed," she said. "Without any argument, as I recall."

She heard the bitterness in her own voice and was sorry for it. She'd been the one to say they should separate, knowing he would choose his loyalty to the sovereigns over her. She hadn't wanted to hear him say it aloud. So she'd been the one to instigate the break. She couldn't blame him for doing exactly what she'd expected, what she'd *known* he would do.

Even though she'd wanted him to argue. Even though she'd wanted him to fight for her, to ignore his loyalty to the king and queen, to ignore everything in order to have her.

Long-festering pain lanced her, her chest tightening under the weight of it. Even as the *Shaerta* rose between them, the longing and need for him so strong she could barely keep from moving into his arms, the hurt of their break brought tears to her eyes.

Appalled by the fact that he probably saw the shimmering wetness, she turned away. She tossed her remaining strips of material toward the couch. "Bind your leg. Bleeding to weakness out of stubbornness won't help either one of us."

She left the sitting room to pace in the large foyer, carefully avoiding looking back at Einar.

CHAPTER FOUR

s Nuala waited on Einar, she checked her own body for injuries she might not have noticed. Her arm ached a little and a large bruise covered her upper biceps and shoulder, but otherwise, no cuts or broken bones.

Her stomach growled as she returned to pacing.

"You're hungry," Einar said.

Surprised by his voice, she spun to face him. He was fully dressed again, his sword strapped back into place. And through the tear in his trousers she could see some of the green-blue silk of a bandage.

"A little," she answered. "What supplies I had fled with my mare."

"I've nothing either, I'm afraid." He glanced at the front door, his scowl forming deep creases in his forehead. "I should have grabbed my saddle pack before we made for the city."

"We didn't know how much time we had or who might be nearby." She might not be able to deal with him on an emotional level. But he was the fiercest warrior in Glengowyn. And he'd helped save her life. She wouldn't allow him to berate his actions in the heat of battle.

She'd never allowed that.

His lips lifted, as if he was remembering the same fact.

And again, Nuala found herself short of breath. Einar was gorgeous when serious, but his smile, rare as it was, left her helpless against his male beauty.

His expression remained soft, the bare smile not faltering as they stared at each other.

Then her stomach growled again. The sound was loud in the quiet foyer and without meaning to, Nuala laughed. Surprised by her own outburst, she covered her mouth. "Sorry," she mumbled around her hand. "I know we need to be quiet."

"In that case, we should feed you or the whole of Sinnale will hear your hunger."

She snorted again into her hand, trying to stifle her amusement. But he smiled a little more at her reaction.

In an attempt to return to the seriousness of the situation, she said, "I can do without for a while. We won't be hiding for long. And besides, where would we find food in Noman's Land?"

"Some humans continue to squat in the buildings closer to Sinnale territory," he said.

But he frowned and she knew he'd considered the same thing she had.

"We won't be any more welcome by them than the border guards because we're unknown elves."

He nodded. "I can go out and scavenge."

"No." Fear tightened her throat. "I don't think we should

separate." Though being around Einar was a kind of torture, letting him go into danger on his own was unacceptable. She didn't care if he was the great and terrible Darkness of Glengowyn. If he got hurt, or worse killed, trying to find her food, she'd never survive it.

He was silent for a long moment. Then, "When I call an owl, I'll see if he might bring us some food."

"So long as it's not a dead rodent." She shivered, only half teasing.

"As you wish," he said so seriously, she burbled out another repressed laugh.

"Until then," he said, glancing at the front door, "rest. Take the sitting room. Try to sleep if you can. It will be a long night."

"And you?"

"I'll wake you in a few hours. You can watch while I rest."

She was afraid he wouldn't sleep, that he wouldn't bother to wake her. He'd been known to remain awake for days in battle and he would consider this a similar enough situation. "Promise me you'll try to sleep, not just rest," she said, even though she knew it was futile.

"I would never promise you anything I might not be able to deliver." His voice dropped to a quiet, deep octave.

The sound sent tremors of tingling sensation through her stomach and down to her core. Again, she wanted to step into him, forgo her duty to Glengowyn, risk her magic, risk everything she was to have him. To lay him on the couch and fuck him until the world ended around them.

Instead, she disappeared into the sitting room. She doubted she'd be able to sleep, but being near him eroded her will, and their situation was too precarious to risk giving in to the *Shaerta*. Or her years of yearning and love.

To Nuala's surprise, she did nap for a bit, blissfully without dreams. When Einar woke her, it was twilight dark. "You let me sleep too long," she accused.

"We can't leave until it's full dark. I'll have time to rest."

She sat up on the couch, a move that brought her level with his groin. Still half asleep, she allowed herself to stare as memories of his thick, perfect cock tormented her. Oh the pleasures they could give each other.

His growl startled her out of her erotic thoughts.

"Don't promise what you have no intention of seeing through," he muttered.

"Don't I?" She was asking herself as much as him. They'd managed to avoid each other's company for two centuries, despite living in the same city. She'd only glimpsed him on the rare occasions she was called to Court, and then there were so many others around, they were safe from this attraction between them.

Now, with no buffers, no royal leaders watching their every move, she was no longer sure she wanted to resist him. Denying herself his love all these years had slowly killed something in her. That something seemed to be stirring back to life. And she wasn't entirely sure she wanted to sacrifice that part of herself again.

Why had the queen and king sent him to guard her? They must have known. Did they really think the centuries would dim her desire for Einar? Why did they tempt them this way if they valued her magic as it was?

She rose. "I'm sorry. That wasn't kind of me. With you…" She waved a hand vaguely in the air, not sure how to explain.

"It's the same for me. With you."

None of the exhaustion he must feel showed in his face, but knowledge that he had to be tired after the fight and the injuries forced her away from their personal desires.

"I'll keep watch. *Try* to sleep." She gave him a level look, which brought out his slight smile, and she gave up. Shaking her head, she picked up her quiver and bow from beside the couch and draped them over her head to rest along her back, then headed toward the doorway and the window at the front door where she could keep an eye on the street.

Before she left the sitting room, though, Einar called her back. "Take my knife. Just in case. Though if you see anyone, let me know immediately."

"I will." She stared down at the knife, thoughts of the elf she'd actually killed rising up.

"I…didn't realize you'd learned to throw knives," he said into the silence.

"I'm not as good as I should be." She shrugged. "Ulric insisted I learn. My talent with bow and arrow notwithstanding, he said I needed a second way to defend myself. Just in case."

"Your cousin is a good man. I'm glad he was able to teach you."

She slipped the borrowed weapon into her belt sheath. "I'll wake you once it's been full dark for a bit. Thank you for the knife."

She was at the doorway when his voice made her pause again.

"He deserved to die, Nuala. Don't regret killing the traitor."

Without turning, she said, "I don't. But the fact that I could, that I had to, makes me…sad."

She left without saying more. This was not the time to discuss her regrets. There were too many anyway.

NUALA CAUGHT SIGHT OF THE SMALL GROUP OF MINIONS while they were a block away. Torn between watching their progress and waking Einar, she decided she had time to wake him.

Slipping on silent feet into the small sitting room, she knelt beside Einar and would have smiled if not for the approaching enemy. He was asleep.

With a soft touch on his shoulder and a finger over his mouth, she murmured his name.

He opened his eyes instantly, coming to full wakefulness without any of the lag time she usually required. Moving her finger from his mouth, she whispered, "Minions approaching from the southeast."

He flowed to his feet, grabbing his sword from where it lay on the floor beneath the couch. Nuala stepped back to give him room then followed him to the windows. The room didn't have any curtains, but it was completely dark inside now. Still, he kept to the wall, deep in the shadows. She used his larger body to conceal herself.

"There," she said when she spotted an individual minion coming into view. They were only a few doors away, but it was obvious they were searching the buildings.

"How did they find us?" she asked.

"How large was the party?"

She shrugged. "There were five when I first saw them."

"Small groups, then. The Sorcerers have probably sent an army of minions into Noman's Land looking for us. Small groups can cover a lot of territory."

"What about the humans patrolling the area?"

"As dangerous to us as the minions right now."

"But won't they…complicate the search?"

Her heart pounding, she watched as two minions entered the building across the street and two doors away.

"Maybe," Einar answered, his voice barely audible he spoke so quietly, "but that won't help us now. We need to get to the roof."

"Is there time?"

He held still for one more heartbeat, then grabbed her hand and tugged, moving swiftly and silently back through the room to the entryway. Without pause, he led her up the stairs, circling around and climbing until they reached the top floor. Once there, they had to search for some way they might access the roof.

Cursing silently, Nuala studied the ceiling down one length of the hall while Einar searched the opposite side of the corridor. When she heard the front door open, she spun to face Einar. He was already moving toward her, faster than most elves could move. He swept an arm around her waist and hurried her to the window at the end of the hall.

He studied it a moment, then opened it as quietly as he could but some noise squeaked out. They froze. The shuffle of feet in the foyer thudded to the stairs.

"*Fateesh*," he cursed and threw the window open, sticking his head out to study their surroundings.

She watched the stairway, his knife in her hand, her entire body tense.

"Onto my back," he ordered in that barely audible whisper.

"What…?"

But he didn't give her time to question his plan. He grabbed her arm just above her elbow and swung her around to his back with a strength that surprised even her. She clung to his neck with one arm, careful not to choke him, slid his knife into one of the scabbards on her belt, then circled her other arm around his chest. She tried wrapping her legs around him high enough to avoid the sword at his side, but the position meant he wouldn't be able to reach his weapon.

In his ear, she said, "Now what?"

He didn't answer. He just climbed into the window frame, crouched so neither of them would bump their heads. Before she could guess at his intention, he leapt, his powerful thighs pushing them off the window ledge and out into the empty air.

CHAPTER FIVE

uala's stomach dropped and it took all her will not to squeal in alarm. She clenched Einar tighter, reflexively, her face pressed into his shoulder as terror slammed through her. The jolt of landing nearly forced her hold to relax. His arm came up and braced her lower back, keeping her from falling.

"Are you okay?" he asked.

She looked around. They'd landed on the roof of a neighboring building, one story below the window they'd jumped from, but far enough away she wouldn't have thought the leap possible. "How?"

"Killing isn't my only skill. You know that."

She unfolded her legs and slid to the ground, stepping away from him before she noticed the contact too much. "Now where?"

He took her hand again and pulled her to the opposite side of the flat rooftop, ducking behind a tall brick chimney just before she heard voices from the window they'd leapt from.

"Anything?"

"No elves. Could they make that jump?"

Silence. Then, "Doubt it. Too far even for an elf."

"The others should go into that building anyway."

"I'll tell them."

"I'll finish here."

Nuala waited in silence for at least ten heartbeats after the voices disappeared, then she raised her brows. Einar nodded. They faced the next neighboring building.

"Me first," he said. "You can make this?"

"Yes." She'd cliff-jumped as a youth, just like the other elves. This distance was at the farthest reach of her abilities but she'd done it before. She held her breath as he made the leap, landing easily and gracefully on the next roof. Then she backed up two steps and threw herself into the jump. When she landed beside him, she laughed, muffling the sound with her hand, but completely unable to contain her reaction to the thrill of making that distance.

He frowned at her. She grinned and shrugged.

"I haven't done that in a while. I forgot how much fun it is."

His frown remained in place but his expression seemed to ease a little. Or at least she thought it did. With the only illumination coming from the two-thirds first moon, it was hard to tell.

Without a word, he led her across the roof to yet another building. After studying the street below, he nodded and they jumped again. She stumbled a little on this landing, the adrenaline of their escape starting to shiver her muscles. The next building down the street was three stories higher than the one they were on, so they turned to the back of the roof and crossed a foot-wide gap to yet another building.

"We'll have to go back to the street," Einar said, searching the surrounding buildings. Two were too high, the other was on the opposite side of the street and still too high for them to jump.

Her stomach danced with fear now that the excitement of building jumping was over.

This roof had an obvious door leading back inside, but Einar paused to study the streets below first. After several tense moments, he joined her at the door, leading her down the stairwell to the ground floor. Nuala barely noticed the building around them. She had a vague impression of square galleries and a multitude of doors, but her full focus was on trailing Einar down the dark stairs, afraid she'd miss her footing if she didn't pay attention.

At the front entrance, Einar paused again, studying the street through the windows beside the door. She had to force air in and out of her lungs. Finally, he eased open the door, which moved on surprisingly silent hinges, and they slipped into the street, sticking close to the building walls.

Sounds from in front of them, the direction they wanted to go, forced them to back-peddle into the alley next to the building, opposite their planned escape route. Einar blocked her view, putting his large frame in front of hers as they pressed close to the alley wall and listened.

The heavy fall of booted feet clicked across the cobbled streets. Listening carefully, she thought she heard two, maybe three different individuals. But since they didn't speak, she couldn't be sure. She and Einar waited for a long while, listening to those boot steps. The sounds faded in and out but there was always at least one person on the road at any given time, making it impossible for her and Einar to go that direction.

She studied the opposite end of the alleyway in frustration. It was a dead end, and at any rate, led them back toward the original group of minions they'd just escaped.

The feel of Einar's breath at her ear made her jump.

"More minions," he said. "Heading away. When I move, don't hesitate."

She squeezed his arm in understanding and turned her focus on his shoulder, braced to run when he did.

As she waited, a sound carried to her across the wind and Einar's back stiffened. She strained to catch more of the noise. Shouts. The clashing of metal. The sharp *swack* of a bowstring releasing. Her heartbeat accelerated.

"A fight, only a street or two over," she murmured. "Sinnale soldiers must have found one of the minion groups."

He nodded in agreement, though he never took his attention from the minions in the street ahead of them. He raised a hand, a silent warning to prepare, and then sprinted across the road. She followed, racing a step behind him. When they made the next alley, he paused and lifted his head, listening.

She could hear it too, more joining the fight. A full-blown skirmish was underway.

"The others are joining the fight," Einar said. "More minions will make their way toward it."

"What do we do? Should we help? Or…"

He shook his head before she could finish. "Sinnale will assume we're traitor elves. Minions will try to kill or capture us. We need to avoid the fight, find another hiding spot."

"The minions will just continue searching. Where can we be safe?"

As he considered their options, they watched another small group of minions race by, heading toward the growing conflict.

"Opposite the fight and toward Sinnale territory," Einar finally said. "As we originally planned. This skirmish is deep in Noman's Land. The Sinnale soldiers are probably all over the area hunting the minions. Neither side will have time to look for two missing elves for hours, maybe not for the rest of the night if the Sinnale win these fights and drive the minions back to Sorcerer territory."

"We'll have to avoid human patrols too," she pointed out.

"They aren't looking for us. We can hide from them. We just need an empty building, no human squatters."

Carefully, and sticking close to the buildings, they made their way through the deserted, ramshackle part of the city that was the buffer between the two warring parties. The occasional gaslamp provided small pools of light, but most of them were dark. And the closer they got to the Sinnale border, the fewer patches of light there were.

Twice they ducked into dark recesses to avoid human patrols. Once they nearly walked out into the path of a minion group. And once they had to change direction to avoid another skirmish. First moon was high overhead by the time they found an empty building that Einar deemed a suitable hiding spot.

Inside, they quietly searched the three levels of the small building, checking for the presence of others likely to return. Every room and corridor was covered in dust that looked undisturbed for months, maybe years. Einar checked the roof as well, assessing possible escape routes. When he was satisfied they were as safe as they could be for the night, he motioned her back inside.

"I'll call an owl. But you'll be more comfortable downstairs."

"I won't be comfortable until we make contact with someone who can help us," she said.

"Still. It's cold tonight. I don't want you to take a chill." He gestured to her torn riding robe. "You've been running and tense. When the sweat cools, you'll notice the cold out here."

"So will you," she said. Then smiled. "And are you trying to tell me I stink of sweat?"

His mouth crooked up at one side, just barely. "You always smell lovely. Go inside. I'll join you shortly."

Giving in, she took the roof stairs to the third floor to scout a suitable room to rest in. They were fortunate that the windows in this building were mostly intact, at least on this floor. Several of the rooms had furniture, though most of it was too filthy to make for comfortable sitting. She found two rooms with beds and one of those beds appeared relatively clean, though it was bare. She studied that room and realized it wasn't as dirty in general as the other rooms, the dust only just starting to accumulate again.

Someone had used that space, not long ago. But there were no signs of it being readied for a return visitor. When she checked the ceramic heater in the corner, there was no kindling or flint and steel to start a fire with. Someone planning on using this room again would have left something behind to start a fire. Or left some clean linens for the bed. She opened the single oak trunk in the room, but it was empty. No, there didn't seem to be signs that whoever had used this room might return. She and Einar should be safe enough here.

With a little sigh, she flipped the mattress over, exposing a dust-free side that was in decent shape, better than she'd expected. Then she sat and waited for Einar.

He didn't leave her alone for long. He filled the doorway when he did join her, his large, muscled frame a paler darkness. Ambient light from both the waning moon and a single working gaslamp gave the room some illumination, but not enough to see his facial expression clearly as he hovered in the shadows.

"Did an owl come?"

He made a noise that sounded like a short, broken laugh. "Of course. They're always happy to answer my requests."

"How do you send messages without anything to write with?" She knew he could do this. He'd done it before. But she'd never asked how he managed. For every other elf, the owls would deliver written notes. Only Einar could deliver a verbal one.

He came into the room, hesitating a few feet from the bed. There was nowhere else to sit, and his hovering rubbed irritatingly against her nerves.

"Sit down, Einar. I won't attack you. We can be in each other's company for a few minutes without succumbing to the *Shaerta*."

Still reluctant, he finally settled on the opposite end of the bed.

"Now. How do you send verbal messages with the owls? I've always wondered and been afraid to ask."

He tilted his head to one side. "You afraid? I find that hard to believe."

"You're avoiding the question."

"The owls can deliver my verbal messages to the king. He's the only other elf who can understand, though he does so in a different manner than I do. He…sees the messages, almost like pictures, from the owl's mind."

"And you? Can you receive verbal messages?" Before he could answer, she let out a half laugh. "But of course you wouldn't know, as the owls won't carry verbal messages from other elves."

"They bring me news that was spoken within their hearing."

She focused on him more fully. "What?"

"While collecting written messages, if they glean information they feel I should know, they tell me. I understand their…language is the only way to describe it. When they speak, I know what they're saying."

"Unlike the king."

"Different from the king."

"What did you ask His Majesty to do?"

"To inform your cousin that we need safe passage from Noman's Land. Once he has a safe way for us to enter Sinnale territory, he can relay that information through the king via the owls."

She released a small breath and smiled. "Ulric. Very clever. Trusted by the humans now. And will recognize us both on sight."

"He'll arrange the proper security so the Sorcerers don't try to infiltrate their territory by pretending to be you and me."

"I hadn't thought of that." She straightened her shoulders.

"A further complication to us just waltzing into Sinnale territory."

"Yes."

"Do they have something or someone who can see through illusion spells?"

"Likely Ulric will impose on the queen. She's the only one of sufficient skill to ensure we're who we say we are."

"Won't that be dangerous for her? If the Sorcerers came after me, surely they'll want the queen when they get word of her coming into Sinnale."

Though the king and queen had both entered the city on several occasions while the elves were technically neutral in the war, they had remained safe in Glengowyn once their support of the Sinnale was made official.

Since Einar was the bodyguard to the royal couple, she was certain he would find the plan too risky. He surprised her by smiling. A full-blown, all-out grin.

"Her Majesty has ways of getting around that most elves are unaware of. She's very purposefully kept a few of her skills a secret. Getting in and out of Sinnale is not as difficult for her as it is for most."

Nuala widened her eyes in surprise. The king and queen had reigned for centuries, so long she'd thought all their magics must have been revealed. Apparently, she was wrong.

"So. We'll see the queen when we finally reach safety."

"I would assume so."

She took in the implications of that for a long moment.

"What are you thinking?" he asked, his voice quiet.

How to tell him? They'd been avoiding this for two hundred years.

Instead of a direct approach, she said, "Why do you think they risk…us on this mission? Together?"

"You're highly valuable to Glengowyn. Who else would they trust with your safety?"

"Ulric."

He dipped his head to the side, a half nod, half shrug. "He would have made an excellent guard. But he's too well known among the Sorcerers now. It was felt his presence would call too much attention to your…importance."

"Many of the traitor elves know you too. Even if they didn't recognize me, seeing the Darkness of Glengowyn would reveal my *importance*." She wanted to sneer the word but kept that reaction to herself. She accepted her position in Glengowyn society, but centuries of the overprotective efforts of the royal couple had left her weary.

She watched Einar carefully as he faced the wall. The soft rise and fall of his chest drew her gaze to the thick muscles. She remembered well how those muscles felt under her hands, pressing against her naked breasts. The weight of him as he covered her. His scent filled her. Mixed with dust and sweat was that distinct spicy musk that was Einar's alone. She'd never met elf or human whose scent called to her the way his did. Unable to resist, she took another deep breath.

Her movements attracted his gaze. Even with him sitting so close, she couldn't read anything in his dark eyes. But she felt the *Shaerta* tickling her skin. His reaction or hers, she couldn't tell. Maybe both. The fire was rising, though. And too much longer on this bed, in this quiet, isolated room, would leave her defenseless to him.

"No one knew I would join the group," he said into the

silence. "Only the king, queen and Ulric. The traitors wouldn't have expected me to leave the sovereigns' side. That gave us an advantage. And while many elves think they know what I look like, most have never looked close enough to recognize me out of context."

She wondered if that was true. Byral hadn't recognized him and Byral had been to Court at least a few times. Maybe fear of the Darkness really did keep the others from looking too closely. She couldn't imagine *not* looking at Einar or knowing every detail of his face. The brush of short hair against his collar and the sharp points of his ears just peeking past the dark, thick waves, the ever-so-slight tilt of his eyes, the firm set of his mouth and solid angle of his jaw. Every detail etched into her heart for centuries.

She blinked and dragged her thoughts back to the conversation. "The traitors did expect me, though," she said. "They knew I was there. They came for me specifically. It wouldn't have mattered if Ulric was with me or not."

"We know that now. They've probably been watching all the caravans, waiting for you to appear. When the plans were made, however, it was thought best to draw as little attention to you as possible while providing you with the highest level of security."

"You."

"Me."

"Did they…" She swallowed as she found herself leaning toward him without meaning to. "Didn't they worry about the *Shaerta*?"

He held perfectly still, not moving closer. Her own weakening will kept her edging across the bed, very slightly, toward him.

"They trusted you to uphold their decree."

"Not you?" That surprised her. He'd been as disciplined at avoiding her as she'd been at avoiding him. Maybe more so. He'd never once shown signs of the weakness she often felt when it came to him.

He didn't answer. Instead, he stood and paced to the opposite side of the room. Then he headed for the door. "I need to check on the skirmishes. I'll be back soon."

He left without a backward glance. Nuala sighed. She removed her bow and quiver and set them beside her on the bed, then leaned on the headboard. Again his willpower managed to stay strong where hers faltered.

But what did she expect? They'd see the queen soon enough. Giving in to the *Shaerta* wasn't an option. While they might be able to get away with a single encounter after all these years, she knew one night with Einar would never be enough. Succumbing to her desires once would make it impossible for her to deny them anymore. Making love to Einar again would ruin her.

And yet, somehow that ruin no longer seemed so bad.

With a groan, she stretched out on the bed to await his return, trying to remind herself why she'd heeded the queen and king's edict in the first place. To ignore their order would lead to banishment for both her and Einar. After so long, that punishment didn't scare her as much. But Einar... She couldn't do that to him. She was sure he wouldn't risk it. Why else had he left the room? He was right. She knew he was. Her value was significant. Banishment would be disastrous for everyone.

But oh how she wanted him to throw caution to the wind,

stalk into the room, strip her naked, and fuck her like nothing else in the world mattered.

A dream, she knew. But a pleasant one that carried her into a light doze as she waited.

CHAPTER SIX

Einar woke her with a gentle touch on her shoulder. Dawn light peeked in through the single window, just enough to see his face clearly.

"Danger?" she asked, half sitting.

"No. We're safe. The fighting moved through Noman's Land most of the night, but the skirmishes shifted toward the Sorcerers' territory and away from us."

"How…?"

He lifted his lips, an almost smile. "The owls."

"Ah. Of course. So…" She sat up completely and looked around the room. Einar straightened and took a few steps back from the bed. "So now what?" she asked. "We wait here?"

"We'll need food and water soon. But for the day, this location should be safe enough."

"I can go without food and water for a bit longer if necessary."

His expression took on a faraway, thoughtful look. "I know. I remember."

She remembered too. The last goblin war had been even harder on them all than the first. In the heat of battle, as she worked frantically to provide enough of her special arrows, she'd often gone for days with only a minimum of food and water. Usually what she got came from Einar's own hands.

"We'll be stronger for any fighting or fleeing if we eat," he said finally.

"There won't be much to find. Not here."

"I've already taken care of it."

"The owls again?"

He dipped his head once in affirmation.

"Very handy, those birds. When they do as you ask."

"It's because I ask nicely."

She snorted. "Of course."

Stretching her arms forward, she loosened her back and shoulder muscles. Then she went to look out the window, carefully standing to one side so she couldn't be spotted from the street.

"No patrols yet this morning?" She kept her face turned away from him as she studied the chunk of city she could see.

"No patrols. From either side. After the fighting, things will likely be quiet for a few hours, at least. Especially since the humans won."

"Did they? I'm glad."

"They drove the minions back behind their own lines. The minions weren't prepared for a full battle."

"And the Sinnale are stronger now. With our help."

Nothing moved on the cobbles below. Not even bits of rubbish blew down the empty alleys and courtyards. The morning air was still and quiet, casting a pink glow that softened the battered buildings and hid the neglect and damage. In that light, she could almost see the city as it had been before the war, a century ago when she'd last been here.

"I'm sorry I can't provide enough water for washing," Einar murmured. "The owls couldn't risk bringing in items too large. Or too many of them flying to the same place. That would give us away."

"It's not a problem. I realize I probably stink." She grinned over her shoulder. "But I can stand it for another day if you can."

The thought of the owls being tracked had her turning to face him fully. "Will they be able to get any supplies to us without attracting attention? Especially in the daytime when they shouldn't really be about except for passing messages. Some lookout somewhere will spot them."

"They can fly low when needs be, avoiding too much attention. But only if there are no more than two or three. More would attract notice."

"Again, I can go without food or water. I wouldn't want to see one of them hurt."

He tilted his head to one side. "I wouldn't risk them unnecessarily."

"I know. I meant… Maybe my comfort isn't necessary enough for their risk."

"Your comfort isn't my concern. Your strength and ability to escape danger is."

How could she argue with that? She looked out the window again, not sure what else to say. Searching for a topic, she recalled one of the questions she'd never broached yesterday. "I forgot until now, but…the Sorcerer who was part of the caravan attack? You said he was never real. What did you mean? I could smell the death stench surrounding him. Even the horses reacted to him."

"He was a...*projection* the king calls it. Difficult and draining magic when so much detail is incorporated. But useful. They send their essence, their spirit, away from their bodies to whatever location they choose, but they aren't there in a form that can be attacked or killed. Their bodies remain safe, probably inside the citadel or their own strongholds. Somewhere within range of the projection location. Ulric noticed them using this technique during the most recent battles with the Sinnale. The Sorcerers can direct efforts and watch the movements of the humans without having to endanger themselves by being physically present during the fight."

"Can these projections cast spells?"

"No. They're limited to observation. That's how I knew the Sorcerer at the caravan attack wasn't real."

Ah. Now she understood. "He would have used magic to stop our escape if he'd been real."

She glanced back at Einar in time to see him nod.

"You said the magic for projection was draining?"

"Very costly to their power stores."

"Then they are weakening by using this spell?"

"Or using up more of their captives toward their magic."

Her shoulders jerked in a shiver she couldn't control. The poor humans. It was no wonder Ulric had been so vocal about bringing Glengowyn into this war. The woman he loved could have been taken and used that way. Nuala couldn't imagine much worse than knowing Einar had been tortured and killed to feed the evil of death magic. Realizing that it could still happen if they didn't reach Sinnale territory safely closed her throat.

She turned back to the window so he wouldn't see her sudden jolt of fear.

As she studied the city and tried not to feel the pull toward Einar that was beyond her control, she began plucking pins from her hair. The tight, battle-ready bun at the base of her head had finally come loose, and the escaped tendrils were itching her neck. She didn't wear her hair this tightly bound often, so her scalp was sore. She set the pins on the windowsill and unwound the bun, leaving the golden-brown braid to fall down her back. She didn't have a brush, and wouldn't have water to rise out the sweat and dust, but even a finger comb would relieve some of the pressure on her scalp.

Removing a final stray pin, she set it with the others, rubbed her fingers across her head, then reached for the strap of leather holding the end of her braid. She jumped when she felt Einar's hands on her shoulders.

The sensation, both familiar and new after all this time, sent a tremor of heat through her belly. With only that brief contact, she could already feel the *Shaerta* rising. Her nerves danced. She drew in a deep breath, absorbing Einar's scent, and the heat in her stomach spread through her abdomen to her core.

Turning to face him just then would destroy what little resistance she had, so she kept her body motionless, her gaze on the street.

He skimmed his hands down the length of her arms, leaving a hot chill along her skin and forcing her hands down to her sides. Then he leaned in and said against her ear, "Allow me."

She wanted to melt into him but couldn't manage any movement, closer or away. He released her wrists and shifted to her braid, untying the leather strap, then slowly separating the strands.

Heart pounding, Nuala closed her eyes, the wash of sensation from having his hands on her overwhelming and perfect. She concentrated on the play of his fingers up her braid, the gentle run of his palms over and through the strands, the heavy fall of weight when her hair was fully freed of its confines, and the merciless thrill of him brushing her hair, his fingers threading over her scalp, pulling the thick locks away from her face. She tilted her head back at his urging, giving him access to better massage her temples. Without realizing she would, she groaned.

"I've missed this," he said, his voice low and deep. "The feel of your hair, your skin."

"I've missed you too," she admitted, despite her best intentions. "I've felt...half of myself for a long time now."

His grip tightened at her admission. Then he released her, and Nuala wanted to cry, knowing he would continue to resist where she could not.

An instant later, she was facing him, his hands tight on her shoulders. His dark eyes sparked in the early morning light, his expression more animated, more desperate than anything she'd ever seen him reveal. Before she could absorb the full impact, his mouth was on hers, firm, strong and so heartbreakingly gentle her entire body relaxed into him.

Einar. After all this time. To taste him again was beyond exquisite, beyond joy. She had no way to put into words the sensation that enveloped her except that it felt like her world finally settled into place and became real.

He cupped her cheeks in his hands, holding her near as his kiss deepened. Still controlled, still luxurious, as if they had all the time in the world for just this kiss. Gripping his waist, she followed him into that place, her tongue brushing and swirling around his, a delicate duel no one would suspect the Darkness capable of. Most thought him hard, emotionless, cold.

She knew better. He was all heat and warmth and emotion. With her, he was passion. And she was free.

Their kiss heated slowly, perfectly. Destroying her and renewing her with each play of lips against lips. He slipped his hands from her face to her waist, snugging her tightly to his body. The press of her breasts against the thick expanse of muscles along his chest weakened her knees. The feel of his cock already hard against her abdomen thrilled her on a deep level. And suddenly all she wanted was the heat of his skin, naked against hers, so she could explore this body she'd been denied for too long.

The *Shaerta* raged through her, heightening her every sense. That underlying musky scent that was Einar filled her head. The touch of his hands, strong on her waist, branded her. The heat of his cock warmed her through her clothes as if there was no barrier between them. And still his kiss was deliberately languorous, deliciously tempting.

Tension flexed his muscles, a tightness echoing her building passion, yet she couldn't rush this reunion any more than he could.

So long, so much time wasted. The reason for their separation no longer seemed to make sense. Not when they had this. Not when she loved him so very much.

Without allowing any space between them, Einar edged

her back toward the bed. She followed his lead, step by step, floating over the dust-covered wood in moments and hours. Her legs touched the mattress and she dropped back, dragging him with her. The drop made them bounce, and despite everything, Nuala giggled.

Einar lifted enough to look down at her, his expression beautifully open. A small smile tugged at his lips, the stone mask he normally wore gone to reveal a tenderness only she was allowed to see.

Reaching up, she cupped his cheek, too touched for words, too happy for regrets.

They would deal with the aftermath of this day soon enough. Now, having him inside her was as vital to her as water and air. More powerful than magic.

With the *Shaerta* riding her, she embraced the consequences, tugging his mouth back to hers.

CHAPTER SEVEN

The first touch of his warm palms on her breasts, even through her clothing, was enough to turn tenderness to desperation. Nuala arched against him, moaning into his mouth. And his grip tightened. Her skin was incredibly sensitive, so that when he found her nipples through her shirt, the tug and pinch was almost painful. She wouldn't have changed a second of that sensation.

But she wanted his hands on her bare skin. Pushing him off, she sat up.

"Nuala?"

The uncertainty in his voice squeezed at her heart. She leaned close again to kiss him, running her hand down his stomach to the thick bulge pressing against his trousers.

"I have no intention of leaving without getting my hands and my mouth on your cock," she said. "I want every inch of you, naked and at my mercy. But I don't want to enjoy you with my clothes on."

Her admission brought more heat to his dark eyes, so

black now they were almost frightening. "I can help with removing your clothing," he said.

Rubbing his cock through his trousers, she shook her head. "You have more important things to do."

He raised his brows.

"Take off your own."

She slid away before he tried to change her mind. Watching him, she unbuckled her belt with Einar's knife in one scabbard and set it gently on the floor. Then she undid the ties closing the front of her robe as he sat up and slipped off his vest and tunic. She allowed herself the freedom to fully appreciate that beautiful chest of his, finally and after so long.

Licking her lips, she dropped her robe and started unlacing the front of her blouse. The heat of his gaze was like a physical touch, a touch she couldn't deny. She opened her shirt, letting the soft material fall down her arms to pool on top of her robe, then quickly pulled off the fitted vest that kept her breasts contained.

He groaned, his gaze locked on her chest as she cupped her breasts and pinched her nipples into hardness.

"You've too much on," she reminded him as she continued to play with herself, knowing how it affected him.

Without taking his gaze from her, he shifted to the edge of the bed to tug off his boots. Rubbing one hand down her abdomen to the top of her riding trousers, she watched him watching her, knowing he wanted to put his hands on her more than he wanted to breathe. Knowing because she felt the same. He stood and shucked off his trousers and underpants, barely paying attention to his own actions.

Because he was doing exactly what she asked, she opened the buttons on her trousers. Then bent to remove her boots.

The forward motion made her breasts sway, and cool air caressed her skin, emphasizing how hot she felt, how deliciously sensitive and ready.

With her boots tossed aside, she straightened and edged her pants down her hips, wiggling a little to free the material. Einar's nostrils flared. He was standing now, as if he hadn't been able to move once he'd stripped. As he watched her reveal the rest of her body, he took his thick erection into his palm and stroked slowly, almost absentmindedly, like he couldn't help himself.

Hunger like she'd never felt swept through her. She wanted her hand on him, her mouth. But she was mesmerized watching him stroke himself. She found herself following his example, letting her fingers dip into her wet curls, stroke through the slick folds of her sex. A shiver took her as she cupped one breast with her free hand.

"I've spent too many nights touching myself and thinking of you," she whispered into the silence, which was punctuated only by their ragged breathing.

"Nuala," he moaned and his fingers flexed around his cock.

"Now, with you watching, I feel whole again. Because I know your hands will be here—" she slid her fingers deeper into her heat, "—taking me, feeling how much I want you."

"You have driven me wild from the first moment we met, Nuala. An insanity I can't regret now."

She smiled and finally allowed herself close to him again. He grabbed the hand she'd used on herself and brought her still-damp fingers to his mouth, sucking the moisture off gently. Her heart thundered, and her knees trembled. Goddess, but he was magnificent. And for this moment, he was hers completely.

Dropping to his knees in front of her, he kissed the skin above her curls, low on her abdomen. Every muscle in her body tightened in reaction, in anticipation. To her relief, he didn't tease her. He mouth dipped lower, over her heat, his tongue licking through her folds and pressing eagerly against her clitoris. She cried out, so sensitive she knew she would come quickly. She didn't care. She would come as often today as he'd allow her. Her fingers shook as she buried them in his short, thick hair and let her head fall back and her eyes close.

He licked and sucked her swollen flesh until she trembled all over, her legs barely holding her upright. The building pressure swelled, consumed, engulfed her until only his mouth on her anchored her to reality. Then the pressure broke and she cried out, despite knowing she should remain quiet. The sound came without thought or permission, a primitive reaction to a release so hard and thorough her knees finally did give out.

Einar caught her before she collapsed, his arms circling around her hips. When she opened her eyes and looked down, he was staring at her, his gaze full of satisfaction.

"I've missed watching you come," he said, his voice deep. "I've never seen anything more beautiful in my long life."

She smiled. "I hope you intend to watch me come a few more times before we're done."

"As often as you can stand," he promised. Then he rose to his feet, his big body enveloping hers as he kissed her again, his hands tight on her waist.

She wrapped her arms around his neck and allowed him to lift her, turning her back to the bed. So much she wanted to do to him. So much she needed from him. As they tumbled to the mattress again, she reached for his cock, delighting in the heat and hardness of him.

His mouth devoured hers now, a man desperate and quickly losing control. She was the only one who'd ever been allowed to see him this way, so unguarded. So close to the edge of a different kind of madness. The privilege of it took her breath away.

Rolling him onto his back, she sprawled across his body, savoring the feel of his naked flesh against hers, so long remembered, so familiar and beloved. The *Shaerta* made every scrape of his chest hair over her breasts, every slide of damp skin against skin, more electric, harder to take and yet impossible to move away from. Overwhelming.

She'd experienced the effect of the hormone with a few other men in her life. But with Einar it was always different— leaving her both desperate and somehow calm when he finally touched her. As if they had from now until time ended to touch, to feel, to pleasure and enjoy each other. It drove her, until she needed to take now, to have him in her, hard and fast and gentle and slow all at once. Pain and pleasure, words too small to describe how she felt with his hands on her, his mouth tasting her.

Remembering this now, feeling it all again, Nuala accepted that she was lost. She would never be able to give this up, to give him up again. Her magic be damned. His duty be damned. This, this heat and need between them, this was a magic all its own, and it would no longer be denied.

Einar's lips slid along her jaw, down to her neck as he tugged her farther up his body. She might have resisted, except she was too needy, too weak to refuse him whatever he wanted from her. When his lips closed hot around her nipple and his teeth scraped the peak, she bucked in response. He held her in place with one hand on her ass as he suckled her breasts, one at a time. The tug started yet another build low in her abdomen, and she ground her hips against his solid stomach muscles in search of relief.

He rose to a sitting position, which let her drop into his lap, his cock nestled between their bodies, and she continued to rub and grind against him. It would never be enough. She needed him inside her. But she was so lost to sensation, she couldn't even demand he fuck her, couldn't speak or control her body enough to take what she wanted. She was helpless to his onslaught, to his pace, his direction.

And somehow, that was perfect.

When he lifted her hips off his lap, she followed, giving him everything she had. The feel of his thickness pushing at her heat became the center of her existence. She tried to drop back to his lap and take him inside her in one swift move, but he held her tight, sliding her down in agonizingly slow increments. She whimpered, unable to help the soft needy sounds as she circled her hips, trying to take him in faster.

Finally, finally he relaxed his grip and she slammed down, filled and stretched and oh-so-much happier. But the satisfaction of having him fully inside her lasted a heartbeat. Then she had to move.

Despite the wash of need and love filling her soul, she rode him slowly, her hips undulating in a rhythm designed to please them both. In this position, she could watch his expression closely, and the intimacy cemented her fall. She was his. She had been from the very beginning of their relationship. And she let him see that now, after all these years, nothing had changed for her.

She loved him. Beyond reason and sense.

He cupped her cheek in one hand while his other stayed firmly on her hip. The emotions in his eyes engulfed her. Kissing him was like oxygen after that, vital to her existence. She continued her steady rhythm, teasing and taking until her body trembled. Then he retook control.

Rolling her onto her back, he built the speed of their coupling slowly at first, increasing the tension tightening her core. Then harder and faster. She clung to him as everything spun away and her reactions took over.

This time, when the release took her, she muffled her cry against his chest, biting down to keep silent. A moment later, she felt him follow her, his body tightening as he came for her.

A pleasure and satisfaction unlike anything she'd known with anyone else lapped over her, leaving her content and savoring a moment she'd remember always.

He hugged her close for a long while after, their breathing slowing together. When he slipped to the side, he gathered her to him, leaving no space between their bodies. His heat seeped into Nuala, keeping her warm despite the chill in the room and the sweat cooling on her body.

In the silence, she wanted to pretend this could last. They could be together with no repercussions. But even her love and contentment didn't allow her the delusion. There would be consequences to this perfection.

She opened her mouth to start a conversation she didn't

really want to have, but stopped when her stomach growled so loudly it echoed in the quiet.

The sound was so unexpected she started to giggle. When she felt Einar's chest bumping her cheek as he tried to suppress his own amusement, she laughed harder. A moment later, he lost control and his deep, uncontrolled chuckle joined hers. He so rarely laughed that the sound enchanted her.

She looked up into his face and smiled. Serious conversations could wait a little longer.

"I guess that means I'm hungry."

"Running across the rooftops then monumentally fabulous sex does tend to do that."

"You experience both together often?"

"Only with you."

She reached up for a kiss.

"The owls should have delivered some food by now. I'll go check." His hand stroked up the length of her bare back. "I want to tell you to stay naked. But…"

His hesitance surprised her. "But?"

"If someone enters the building while I'm on the roof, I don't want you to be vulnerable."

She cupped his cheek. "I'm not vulnerable without clothes. Except with you. But if it will make you more comfortable, I'll dress while you're gone and strip immediately after you return."

That earned her another of his glorious smiles, this one sexy and deliciously wicked. "I do prefer keeping the sight of your beautiful body to myself. I'll be quick."

He was out of bed and dressing so fast, she giggled again. As he hurried out the door to the roof, she tugged on her trousers and shirt, not bothering with the niceties of undergarments or her riding robe. She wouldn't be keeping these clothes on long enough for that.

She did, however, uncover her scabbard belt from the pile of clothes and remove Einar's knife. She only noticed then that he'd moved her bow and quiver to lean against the wall near the head of the bed. She'd been so caught up in their passion, she'd forgotten she'd left them on the mattress.

After a brief hunt in the room next door, she uncovered an empty, thankfully intact chamber pot and took advantage of the find. Then she went to stand by the window in their room and study the street carefully while she waited for Einar to return. As before, everything was silent, giving the area an abandoned feel.

Likely, this part of Noman's Land *was* abandoned. Or any squatters were hiding and asleep. She'd never stopped to consider if the Sorcerers attacked during the day or kept their movements restricted to the night. There was no reason they wouldn't be about during the day, not that she could think of, but the utter silence of the morning hinted that everyone had huddled back behind their lines to wait for... something.

She didn't look away from the street when she heard Einar return, giving the area a final sweep, just in case. Silence and stillness reigned.

"I didn't see anything from the roof either," he said quietly. "We have more time. To rest."

She faced him. "I hope you intend to do more than just rest with me."

He lifted three small sacks. "I also intend to feed you."

Sidling toward him, she set the knife onto a locker beside the bed and without pausing opened her shirt and let it slip off her arms to the floor. His gaze dropped to her breasts as her nipples puckered in the cool air.

"Only food?" she asked as she tugged her trousers off with equal speed and lack of ceremony. The increasing rise and fall of his chest as his breathing sped made her shiver.

"Not just the food," he confirmed to her satisfaction. When he met her gaze, both amusement and heat flickered in his dark eyes. "But you need to eat and drink before any other activities."

"Hmmm. Maybe."

Though the water did sound very good at the moment, the feel of Einar's chest against her palms seemed more important. The *Shaerta* continued to spark and fizzle in her blood. They hadn't been apart long enough for it to ease. And it drove her beyond other bodily needs.

But when he drew out a water sack, thirst did reassert itself, and she gulped down a heavy few swallows gratefully. He made sure she was drinking before uncorking a second sack for himself. Watching the way his throat worked as he swallowed amplified the building heat between her legs.

Though she knew she couldn't afford to waste drinking water on cleaning herself fully, she retrieved one of the remaining strips of silk she'd cut for bandages from her robe and poured just enough water onto it to wash her most intimate parts.

Einar watched, still as a statue, while she caressed the damp silk over her swollen flesh, between her legs. His focused attention started her heart beating rapidly, and the excitement already a low hum in her veins thrummed.

"You're more beautiful than anything I've ever seen," he said, his gaze locked on her gentle movements.

She wanted to tell him she loved him too. But she held back, knowing that declaration would require a serious conversation. And in that moment, she didn't want talk.

"You're overdressed," she commented as she set the strip of silk aside and reached for the remaining two burlap sacks, each holding enough food to see them through the day.

She investigated their food while watching him strip from the corner of her eye. He was already hard, much to her pleasure. The sight kept her breathing erratic, even when her stomach rumbled again as the scent of strong cheese rose up to her.

The owls had brought them a round of Glengowyn cheese, two small loaves of bread and some dried fruit and nuts. Lightweight but substantial enough to keep up their energy for the night ahead.

Though, given the energy they'd just used, and were about to use again, they probably could have done with another round of cheese.

Despite his obvious desire and the gentle bump of his erection against her hip, he did make sure she ate some of the food first, popping a small bite of cheese between her lips while she was too distracted by his nearness to think.

She chuckled and allowed him to feed her, savoring the care, the attention. While her people coddled her because of her magic, no one but Einar ever thought to really take care of her in so fundamental and loving a way.

During the second goblin war, he'd done the same, ensuring she ate and drank, watching until he was satisfied she'd consumed enough to continue working. And her awe, the power of the gesture, came from the fact that he didn't pay any attention to who witnessed his care for her. He didn't try to hide how he looked out for her.

The most deadly and dangerous elf of Glengowyn, the warrior singlehandedly responsible for the deaths of hundreds, maybe thousands of enemies, so feared even his fellow soldiers stepped carefully around him, took the time to care for her and only her. The contrast and his lack of concern for what others thought of his actions were the tipping points for her, the moments that sent her from desire into a deep love she'd never been able to overcome.

After making sure she ate enough cheese and bread to keep her stomach from growling again, she insisted Einar eat as well. It didn't escape her that he didn't eat while he focused on her. So she returned the attention, making him sit on the bed as she handed over chunks of cheese and dried fruit. Only when she was satisfied he'd had enough to curb his own hunger did she allow him to set the remaining food aside and take her into his arms.

His kiss was hard, with an edge of desperation, as he pressed her back into the mattress. As if the short time they'd been apart had seemed longer. He cupped her breasts in both hands and she arched beneath him, moaning into his mouth when he pinched her nipples into hard little peaks. He wasn't rough, but he wasn't delicate with her either. And the strength of his callused fingers rubbing over her skin drove her wild.

She reached for his cock, but he grabbed her wrists and stretched them up over her head, pinning her with one large hand while the other returned to her breast.

He kissed his way along her jaw to her ear and murmured, "You can touch soon. But I need my fill first." Then he gently bit her lobe.

She shivered in reaction. Her ears were actually quite sensitive—most elves' were—but Einar knew exactly how much pressure, how much pain to inflict to bring her the most satisfaction. Using his teeth, he tugged her lobe just enough to make her gasp, then nibbled his way down her throat, savoring her skin.

Almost without meaning to, she jerked her hands against his hold, the desire to return his caresses, to run her nails across his skin was so strong. He held her in place easily, and his strength, his control of her body might have been intimidating from any other man. But with Einar, she felt safe and loved, even as he drove her to mindless desperation.

His mouth slipped across her collarbone and then his lips replaced his fingers on her breast, sucking the sensitive skin hard. Her hips bucked, rubbing his erection. He growled but didn't release her nipple or her wrists.

Nuala's skin sparked with sensation as he shifted to her other breast. She watched him as he licked her nipple in a slow circle, his focus on her body so complete it was breath-stealing. The wet slide of his tongue, the suck and tug of his teeth made the muscles of her stomach quiver. She wanted his mouth lower, yet she didn't want him to stop his current torture, so she bit her lip and closed her eyes, concentrating on the feel, the sensations dancing over her.

He released her wrists only when he dipped lower. She started to lift her arms, but he ordered, "Don't move."

She complied even though she was desperate to touch him. Then he kissed across her waist, along her sides, and she clenched her jaw to keep from screaming. Her skin was beyond sensitive now, and again she rode the edge of pleasure just a hair short of pain. It took what little restraint she had to keep her arms in place above her head, but letting him take whatever he wanted from her, as he wanted it, was a heady sensation she found intoxicating.

She watched him when she could keep her eyes open, trembling as his lips glided across her hip bone, his tongue licking into the crease between her thigh and pelvis. She couldn't control the way her body writhed under his touch, but he held her hips and kept her in place for the torture.

His breath was warm over her damp curls, turning her ragged breaths to pants as anticipation tightened her muscles. She felt stretched and too hot. So that when his mouth finally closed, hard and demanding over her wetness, she barely held a scream back.

He licked through her folds and dipped his tongue deep into her, mimicking the slide of his cock. She dug her fingers into the mattress above her head to keep from reaching for him. The play of his lips and tongue, working her skin, circling and sucking her clit while she was unable to touch him forced her full focus on his attentions.

Every part of her drew down to a tight center, aided by the brush of cool air over her puckered nipples, the tight grip of his fingers on her ass as he lifted her hips to better his access. She was completely open to him, at his mercy, and knowing he wanted her there drove her past restraint.

She came against his mouth, her hips bucking, her body jerking out of her control. When he continued to lick her, she did cry out, too sensitive to remain quiet.

With the *Shaerta*, her body felt like an exposed nerve. She was overly sensitive and afraid she couldn't take much more. And yet she did. He forced her into another, almost painful climax, this one deep and resonant.

He didn't give her time to come down from her orgasm before he replaced his mouth with his cock, rubbing the tip of his erection through her folds, teasing, taunting. He stared at the place where their bodies came together, and she followed his gaze, unable to look away as he held himself at her entrance without actually sliding in. She wanted to beg, plead for more, but she couldn't find her voice.

His expression and focus were fierce, and all for her. That more than anything allowed her to take his torture. But she couldn't stop her hips from jerking in a vain attempt to force him closer.

When he finally pressed the heavy, thick tip of his erection just inside her, she jerked again. He looked up, his eyes dark as he held her gaze.

"Mine," he growled, his voice a harsh pant.

"Yes," she answered, though only a hint of sound got through her clenched teeth.

He eased inside her another inch. The slow entrance kept all her attention on her own body and what he was doing to her. She couldn't get away, couldn't distract herself with any other sensations. He forced her to feel each inch of his cock, the stretch of her passage, the friction of his velvet-hard skin pushing deeper. Never had she been so aware of every jump and sizzle of her nerves, every brush of air, each pulse of her heartbeat. So that when he finally filled her fully, she was almost ready to come again.

He set a steady, deliberate rhythm, pulling almost out before sliding back in. He didn't move fast, he didn't fuck her hard, he kept to a relentless pace that drew out more sensation than if he'd slammed into her. And her orgasm this time was so deep, so complete, so long, she lost all sense of the world around her, of everything but Einar.

By the time she came back to herself, his mouth was on hers, his kiss both sweet and desperate as he finally increased his rhythm, pounding hard to an orgasm she felt along every inch or her own body. He pumped into her several strokes after he came, as if he was no more in control of his body than she was of hers.

She took advantage of his release to finally lower her arms, bringing her hands to his face, holding him there as she savored the brush and play of his tongue with hers. Finally, he lifted onto his forearms and looked down at her. The love, the intensity in his expression was worth everything to her.

Whatever the future held for them, she would hold this moment and his love close to her soul forever.

They spent the rest of the morning in soft caresses, eager kisses, heat and powerful need. Nuala indulged all the desires she'd kept locked tight in her heart for the long centuries, sucking, licking, tasting, fucking, savoring every inch, every ounce of his body. They barely spoke, and while she didn't know why he remained quiet, she knew for her part, she didn't want to risk breaking the spell, allowing reality to intrude on this ideal time. To speak would be to admit her love, to admit things had changed and there was no going back.

So silently she loved him, pleasured him and allowed him to be her world for the few hours they had, the only time they might ever have once news of their fall reached the king and queen.

She buried that fear deep, hiding from it while she anchored herself to the present and her love for Einar.

CHAPTER EIGHT

Nuala rolled into Einar's arms after a light doze, feeling rested and sated in her soul. He stared down at her, his dark eyes thoughtful, his expression quiet.

And now what? she thought. She loved him. They'd defied their king and queen. Already she could feel the threads connecting them binding tighter. They couldn't stop the process now. The *Shaerta* was too strong between them. A reaction only possible when two were in love. She'd managed to step away from this love once. Now, that was no longer possible.

"We'll be banished," she said, surprised how matter-of-fact her tone was, how easy it was to say aloud after avoiding those very words for the last few hours.

He nodded.

"Will they…?" She swallowed. "Will they impose the *Or'roan?*"

She was no different from the other elves. The thought of ending forever, of joining the traitor she'd killed in black nothingness, terrified her. Never to move on to the next plane or see another life… Horrifying prospect. It was why the punishment was so powerful among her people. They all feared it. Which was one of the many reasons the sovereigns had imposed the *Or'roan* on the traitors.

And by loving the Darkness and risking her magic, she'd put both herself and Einar in the same position as the traitors.

"They may," he said after a quiet moment. "Mainly as a statement to others who might dare to defy them. It depends on how angry they are with us."

"We've never been sure how this would affect my magic. Maybe it won't be so bad? Maybe they won't have to punish us, after all."

Desperate dreams, she knew. The queen had made her position on this clear when she'd ordered Nuala to stay away from Einar, to never bond with him. There would be no mercy.

His firm mouth tilted up at one corner. "We'll be banished. But maybe they'll resist cursing us. Either way, you're worth it to me."

Her throat tightened with emotions she tried to suppress. Though why she felt the need to hold anything back with Einar, she wasn't sure. "As long as I'm with you, even if we can't travel to the afterworld together, I'll be happy."

He gathered her close and kissed her.

At sundown, they dressed and returned to the roof, hiding behind the parapet as they studied the streets. Noman's Land had been quiet all day, something that surprised Nuala. She'd expected at least a human patrol after the night of fighting. But the streets remained eerily silent. Not even random squatters or sentries made themselves known.

They waited for a carrier owl until well after full dark, silently keeping vigil. She wanted to talk more, to make sure he was prepared for the consequences of what they'd spent the day doing. Could he really just abandon all he'd ever stood for—Glengowyn, protecting the sovereigns, defending his people? All of that…for her?

And there were his inner demons, the topic they'd avoided all this time. The brutal killer he became in battle. Some called him a berserker. She knew that wasn't the right description. He wasn't overwhelmed by bloodlust, killing indiscriminately. What happened to Einar was scarier, colder, more methodical. A type of battle madness never seen before among the elves.

There was no name for it. But the berserker title added weight to his position as bodyguard to the royal couple, so he didn't try to deny the rumor. Neither did he comment on the suspicion that he was the only elf capable of killing other elves. She knew better than that too—from her own experience now. But again, the whispers added to his legend. Something she was sure the queen and king encouraged.

Beyond the legend and rumors surrounding the Darkness, though, there *was* a violence in Einar, just under the skin. Whatever it was that made him so terrifying a warrior. Would he be able to bank that part of himself for a quiet, isolated life with her?

Banishment would mean they wouldn't be welcomed in any elf city on the planet. And any human city that traded with elves would shun them as well. Their only possible choice would be isolation somewhere out of the way of everyone. But could he survive that?

Could she?

She'd told him the truth. So long as they were together, she could survive anything and be happy. She knew he loved her, even without words. But would he feel the same way after a century of solitude?

The barest of movements from Einar brought her to full alert. Barely visible in the light from the two-thirds first moon and the single gaslamp working on that block, she made out the white ghost of a messenger owl, gently gliding toward them. Einar remained seated but raised his arm to provide a perch for the bird.

She opened her mouth to protest. He wasn't wearing protective leathers. The bird's claws would slice his arm. But a moment later, the owl alighted and somehow avoided digging its talons into Einar's vulnerable skin.

"How…?" she murmured.

He smiled but his gaze was focused on the bird. "My arm seems to be resistant to injury. Part of the way my magic works."

"Amazing." She watched him with the owl, taking advantage of a rare opportunity to witness him with the creatures he was so tied to, his unique magic.

Some thought his fighting skills were enhanced by magic also. Einar had never confirmed or denied that. The king and queen probably knew. The queen had a skill for identifying talents. But the owls, that was definitely a kind of magic. Watching him this closely with them was fascinating.

After a long silence, Einar finally opened his mouth and a soft whispery sound came out. Not at all what she was anticipating. She'd half expected him to screech like the owls. His whisper was mixed with very faint whistles. And then the owl launched upward, its powerful wings fanning her face with cool air as it gained height and angled back toward Glengowyn.

"So," she said. "Do we have safe passage?"

He nodded but his gaze remained on the retreating owl. "Ulric and the queen will meet us at a sentry point at the border at dawn."

"Dawn? Why not now?"

"No explanation was given. We'll have to make our way toward the meeting point well before dawn to make the appointed time, but we have to stay hidden for most of the night."

"How will we know where to go? Is it a location you're familiar with? Can you be sure it won't take us most of the night to get there?"

"The owl provided an aerial map of the area so I can find the sentry point. And he flew the most direct route so I could judge the required time. That route wouldn't take us long, but I doubt we'll be able to travel easily. The owl spotted at least one minion patrol near that area. There will be more."

"Then we won't be able to wait here?"

"Probably not. They'll be looking for us again."

She stared out over the streets, surprised the idea of leaving this little island of quiet made her sad. It wasn't exactly luxurious accommodations. But it had kept them safe through the day and given them a place to be together again. Leaving meant facing reality and consequences.

Einar gripped her chin and turned her face back toward his. He was closer now, his gaze direct when he said, "We'll face what we must together. I won't let the Sorcerers have you."

"And what of the queen?"

"She won't take you away from me either. Not again."

Her breath shivered out of her, but she firmed her shoulders and pushed back the worry. "When should we leave?"

He studied the street below, and she watched the side of his face as he thought and considered. Finally, he nodded as if confirming something to himself.

"We'll leave now, go slowly and carefully. I don't want to get caught far away from the meeting point at dawn because we were forced by minion activity to move in the opposite direction."

"What if there's no safe place nearby to wait?"

"We'll find something." He looked back at her. "You only have two arrows left. Keep my knife with you and don't hesitate to use it, on minion or elf."

She swallowed. "It wasn't as difficult as I thought it would be, killing the traitor yesterday."

"No. It isn't. Some deaths are easy to mete out."

"But I'm not you."

He touched her cheek with the tips of his fingers before dropping his hand. "And I'm very grateful for that. You are, however, noble and just. Your actions come from that part of you. Not the place where my abilities come from."

Because he'd broached the subject, she asked, "Will banishment…make things…difficult for you? In that regard."

Tilting his head, he frowned as if she'd asked him something nonsensical. "I would welcome a reprieve from the Darkness."

"But for how long?"

"To be with you? Forever."

Her throat tightened again. In that moment, with the *Shaerta* still a tangible thing between them, he could speak of forever and no regrets. He could be sure the violence that made him who he was would just go away. But, for his sake, she couldn't afford the luxury of that assurance. She didn't push him further though. They had to survive the night.

And face the queen.

They collected the remaining fruit from their food stores and the little bit of water in their sacks, strapped on their weapons and left their sanctuary as carefully and quietly as they'd entered it that morning.

A cold breeze hummed through the city, kicking up dust and debris from the cobbles. She tugged the remains of her riding robe tighter around her and followed Einar through the shadows, keeping her attention on the streets and alleys at their back while Einar focused on what was ahead.

They traveled slowly, sticking to the deepest dark pools at the sides of buildings and in narrow passageways. Most of Noman's Land remained black, with only the occasional gaslamp to provide any light, so staying to the shadows was easy enough. As they skirted one of the rare lit lamps, Nuala couldn't help but wonder who was lighting them, the humans or the Sorcerers.

The first sounds of booted feet sent them down a side road, into a blackness between buildings she had trouble navigating. She kept a hand on Einar's lower back so she wouldn't lose him and allowed him to lead her to a more open street a block away.

While waiting to make sure their way would be clear, he leaned in and said, "That sounded like humans. But farther away, I heard carriage wheels."

That made her frown. His hearing was significantly better than hers, despite how acute hers was, but that wasn't what bothered her. Why a carriage in Noman's Land? What were they moving that couldn't just walk? And who was moving the mysterious something? A carriage was too easy to hear, too easy for two lone elves to hide from. It made no sense to bring something so awkward and noisy into a search, if the carriage belonged to the Sorcerers, not when there were more than enough minions to scour the streets on foot. And she couldn't think of a single reason the Sinnale might send a valuable carriage into Noman's Land.

"Stay alert," Einar said, then led her across the open street to yet another set of quiet shadows circling what had once been a greenery-filled square.

They edged through the blocks so slowly, so carefully, it felt as if the journey that should have taken a short time took half the night. Nuala's muscles remained tense as she kept alert for movement and sound. Maintaining that kind of vigil wore on her, and exhaustion crept through her body with the passing minutes.

As they waited, yet again, while Einar assured himself of their way, she rubbed her shoulders in an attempt to release some of the tension and pressure. She'd be no good in a fight if her body was already too tired to react because she'd gotten tight from containing her fear.

The goblin war had been... Not easier. Still tense, still

exhausting. But the constant action and battles had kept her too busy to spend much time thinking and worrying. There were only a few quiet moments, a few brief respites during which to consider the fear in her gut. And Einar had always distracted her with conversation during those quiet times. This was different. Though they were moving, the tension of hiding and remaining silent while others hunted for them didn't keep her from thinking and considering the worst.

She would not allow the Sorcerers to take her. Or to kill Einar, if she could help it. Unfortunately, she was woefully undertrained for a fight, and she kept imagining Einar's death. Even the thought clogged her throat and brought tears to her eyes. To actually see such a thing…

Rolling her shoulders, she pulled in a deep silent breath, held it, then let it out slowly through her nose, releasing the building panic. So far, they'd avoided the various patrols—both human and minion. They were nearing the rendezvous point. Safety was in sight. They'd both survive this.

Einar held their position for longer than at any other part of their journey, his body so still she reached out to touch his back just to assure herself he was breathing.

Leaning in close, she said, "What's wrong?"

He held up a hand for silence. After another torturous few moments passed, he turned and spoke into her ear, his voice barely audible. "Minions have surrounded the area near the meeting point. Several contingents. Something has given the location away."

"Where?" she mouthed, knowing he would hear without her having to make more than the barest of sounds.

"In the buildings. On the rooftops. I've spotted them in at least three different locations, so far. The center of their positions is the sector of Sinnale border where Ulric is supposed to meet us."

"Will the humans come if there are so many minions waiting?"

He didn't immediately answer, and his silence made her already jumping heartbeat speed.

"They may be there already," he finally said. "That could be why so many minions have gathered. But we're not close enough for me to see."

"They'll wait for us. They won't start fighting yet."

"There's some time before dawn. We're not safe here, but I can hear minions moving in behind us."

His comment startled her. She directed her attention back to the area they'd already passed through, and now she could hear the faint sound of marching, several blocks away but moving swiftly in this direction.

They were surrounded.

CHAPTER NINE

"Now what?" Nuala said, leaning closer to Einar as the tension that had carried her through the streets turned to full-fledged fear.

He stared up at the sky as if in thought, and because she trusted him, she didn't interrupt. But the sound of approaching footsteps sent her pulse racing. She slipped her bow over her head, readied one of her two remaining arrows, and faced the path behind them, watching their backs.

An intolerable few moments passed in silence and anticipation of attack, reminding her of their ride in to Sinnale and the knowledge that they *would* be attacked at some point in their journey. Then Einar sucked in a deep gulp of air.

"We'll have help in a moment," he said against her ear.

She frowned up at him, about to ask what help, when slight movement from the corner of her eye made her pause. She looked toward the sky. Past some of the lower rooftops, she caught flashes of white, gliding silently in their direction. It took her a beat to realize what she was seeing. Owls. A lot of them, approaching in a fast, silent mass from the direction of Glengowyn.

She gripped Einar's arm. "They'll be hurt."

"Watch. And follow my direction."

She kept her gaze on the approaching birds, the readied bow and arrow in hand. The mass swished overhead, silent except for the beat of their wings. In that pass, a few shouts rose from the surrounding buildings, and Nuala spotted a number of minions pointing toward the sky. To her horror, she watched as one drew back the string on his bow. But before he could fire, something dark dropped from the sky, hitting him on the very top of his head. The man collapsed without even a shout to indicate he was hurt.

Nuala looked up to see even more owls, circling above the area. One by one, they dropped low, released something from their talons, then climbed quickly back to join the others. More shouts rose from around them, echoing through the streets. Arrows launched into the sky, but the owls kept high and beyond their reach. And then another volley of arrows filled the air, this one aimed at the rooftops, toward the minions.

Chaos erupted then. Arrows flew. The sound of swords clashing rang. Minions poured out of the surrounding buildings as human soldiers charged into the streets. A full-blown assault filled the early hour before dawn with noise and madness.

"This helps us?" she asked Einar as she glanced back toward the owls. The mass of white circled farther away, near enough to return if needed but well beyond the reach of the combatants' weapons.

"We can move through chaos. Without this, we were dead."

She hoped he was right. But when he stepped out from their cover and into the street, toward the fighting, she didn't hesitate to follow. His sword in one hand, he edged her through the conflict, easing them toward the border. She kept her bow readied but angled down. With only two arrows and a knife, she had to be careful how she used her weaponry.

A minion spotted them and turned to attack, only to be cut down by a human soldier before she could speak. The human stared at them a moment, and then was distracted by more minions.

"We're in as much trouble from the humans out here, aren't we?" she shouted to be heard above the cacophony.

"Yes. We need to find Ulric."

Their path was blocked by three minions, all of them with a blank, dead look on their faces. The lack of emotion didn't take away from the wicked-looking edges on their blades. They attacked en masse, and Einar met them, sword raised. Nuala put her back to a wall and kept an eye on the fighting behind them, ready to use those last two arrows.

She jumped when a hand grabbed her wrist, but recognition of that touch sank in before she even faced Einar. He tugged her farther up the street, passing the three minions he'd killed so quickly.

They ducked into doorways to let individual fights slide past and edged around what they could. When minions attacked them directly, Einar dispatched them. Only one or two humans made an attempt to reach them, but each time they were turned away by minions. Since Nuala didn't want to risk having to kill a Sinnale, she was grateful the battle chaos prevented any humans from getting to them.

As they neared the border, the fighting grew thicker, heavier. The volley of arrows more dangerous. They kept to cover, but several missiles clattered near their feet. Nuala clenched her jaw tight to keep from screeching in surprise. The battle grew too thick to navigate, and Einar was forced to engage more enemies, beating a swath through the swarms of bodies.

She covered his back, keeping close enough to follow but far enough away to prevent hindering him. She used her last two arrows efficiently to end a charge by three minions. Then she turned to the knife, slicing a threat when anyone got too close. But Einar was a force in battle, unlike anything most of these humans had seen. And it was all they could do to avoid his blade.

Unfortunately, the current of the fighting pulled him too far away, and suddenly she was alone and surrounded by dead-eyed minions. The stench of rot that clung to them wafted toward her. At the edge of the circle, humans continued to pick their former city mates off one by one, but the four that focused on Nuala approached without pause.

She raised the knife, preparing to defend herself. Above the screams and clashes of metal, she heard her name bellowed. Beyond the approaching four, she saw bodies actually flying through the air to slam into brick walls. Einar. Becoming the warrior so feared by elves and goblins.

The four closing in on her didn't realize the Darkness was coming for them.

Two of them vanished so quickly from in front of her she didn't even see Einar take them. One moment they were there, the next they were gone. The remaining two continued forward as if they didn't notice the others had disappeared. The nearer they got, the stronger that faint hint of decay that emanated from them grew. The scent had surrounded her as they'd worked through the crowds, but now she seemed to home in on it, a primal part of her recognizing the meaning and gagging at the thought of the twisted magics that caused that smell.

From the surrounding madness, Einar appeared. He plucked up one of the remaining two attackers and launched him into the nearest group of fighters, sending all of them into a crumpled heap of bodies—Sinnale and minion alike.

Nuala gasped. She hadn't seen Einar like this in centuries. And then only once, because she'd been so carefully kept back behind the front lines. A small group of goblins had tried to infiltrate their camp, purely by chance stumbling across her tent. The elf warrior who came to her rescue was like nothing Nuala had ever seen. Cold, focused madness, speed and a kind of anger that cut down all in its path.

When the goblins had been slaughtered, singlehandedly, and Einar stood barely breathing heavily in the aftermath with blood dripping from his sword and body, his reputation as the Darkness was sealed for all time. Those who'd witnessed the destruction he'd wrought would never forget that sight.

Nuala never had. Seeing him in that same state of cold rage now spiked her pulse and sent a new kind of fear through her. Fear for him and what this might do to him. She knew this would cost him, cost his soul. She was probably the only one who did. And yet she was awed by the sight, the beauty of something so deadly, so powerful...protecting her.

The fourth minion was a bloody splotch on a nearby

building before he fully turned to face the danger. Einar roared and those near him fled, both human and minion. The sound even made the hairs on Nuala's nape rise. Though the fighting continued, it moved away from them, leaving them in a circle of calm emptiness.

He faced her and she watched him physically work to control himself, to return to a more natural state. His eyes were black. Blood ran in rivulets across his face and body. The thought that some of that might be his sent her to his side. No other elf would approach him like this. But she knew he'd never hurt her.

"Are you wounded?" she asked, examining him with her eyes and hands without waiting for his answer.

"Nothing of consequence."

"This is mostly their blood then." She confirmed that with her cursory exam. "Good."

Her comment seemed to surprise him, though she wasn't sure why, and the last of the battle madness eased from his eyes.

"You aren't hurt?" he said, his voice rough.

"Of course not. You didn't give them time to get close. Thank you. I'm not that good with the knife." She touched his cheek. "I'm sorry for this, though."

Before he could answer, a scream of attack rose up to invade their circle of solitude. Einar spun to face the threat, pushing her behind him. But before the minion closed, an arrow thwacked into his chest, directly through his heart. He hit the ground face first, sword still raised above his head. The fall broke the arrow and the puff of a dying spell reached out to tap at Nuala's magic.

An elf arrow. She looked toward the alley from which the

arrow had flown just as another elf approached them from farther up the street. Not a traitor this time, though. Nuala's shoulders relaxed.

"Ulric."

Her cousin greeted them with a sharp nod, and he and Einar grasped wrists in a soldier's solute.

"You're well, both of you? Injuries?"

"Nothing significant. We must get her to the safety of the border." Einar wasted no time with pleasantries.

From the alleyway Nuala had been half watching, a Sinnale woman approached, her bow in hand but without an arrow nocked in place. She was a striking woman, with short brown hair, sharp features and deep brown eyes.

Einar looked at her in surprise then said to Ulric, "You allowed her into battle? I thought…"

Ulric rolled his eyes and the woman smirked. "I had very little say in keeping her away. Stubborn woman."

The woman introduced herself to Nuala. "I'm Layla Brightarrow. It's truly a pleasure to meet you in person, Nuala of Glengowyn. Your cousin has sung your praises."

"Ulric's mate." Nuala understood the surprise. Ulric was so protective of his mate, Nuala hadn't even met her yet, though the woman had been to Glengowyn several times to negotiate for weapons. Obviously, Nuala had drawn the wrong conclusions—she'd assumed by Ulric's protectiveness that Layla wasn't much of a soldier. But this thin, tall woman held the bow like it was part of her. And she didn't look at all shaken by the chaos.

"I understood you'd given up fighting," Nuala said to cover her surprise, "in favor of weapons trade."

Layla glanced at Ulric and shrugged. "I have. I can do

without this death and killing. But you represent our chance to end this war once and for all. I'd hardly stay safe while you were in danger."

The human's declaration made Nuala feel both pleased and little hurt, though she wasn't sure why the hurt.

"Besides," Layla finished with another half-smile, "I couldn't wait to meet a relative of Ulric's that he actually likes."

Ulric scowled and sniffed as if this was a subject he'd rather not discuss. Nuala couldn't blame him. They'd both been baffled and hurt by Althir's turning traitor to join the Sorcerers. She still had trouble believing it of him. Althir was many things—vain, too charming, arrogant, rude, impossible and jealous of Ulric—but she'd have sworn he was loyal to Glengowyn above all else.

Einar brought the small group back to the issue at hand. "We need to make for the border. The queen…"

"Has already confirmed who you are. Though after…" Ulric waved his hand at the smashed and bloody heaps of bodies Einar had left in his wake. "After witnessing the Darkness in action again, there could hardly be doubt."

"The queen is here?" Nuala asked, a tickle of dread curling in her stomach.

"She returned to Glengowyn just after the battle got underway."

"Then how?" Nuala glanced between herself and Einar. How could the queen have confirmed their identity for Ulric before even seeing them?

"The owls," Einar answered, surprising her.

"Ah." Between the presence of the owls earlier to confirm Einar was near and witnessing the release of the Darkness just now, it would be hard for Ulric to doubt him. And if Einar claimed she was Nuala, no one would argue the point. Though her cousin might have been fooled by a Sorcerer's spell, Einar would never be when it came to her. The queen would know that.

"The queen also sent out a *reaching* to make sure there were no glamour spells in the center of the owls' attack," Ulric continued. "She sensed only you and Nuala."

So the queen had been comfortable confirming their identity, sight unseen. Part of Nuala was more than a little relieved. But an edge of anxiety, waiting for the confrontation with the sovereigns to finally come, kept her from relaxing.

The sounds of conflict, though farther way, were starting to quiet.

"Come," Ulric said. "The border is just beyond that block. There's a line of soldiers waiting to defend our backs. But…" He glanced off toward the sound of retreating battle. "But I think we've beaten them back for the night. The sight of you in all your battle anger probably terrified even the minions."

Einar didn't comment. He just took Nuala's arm and followed Ulric and Layla to the border. He didn't return his sword to his scabbard, and she didn't put away her knife, until they were well behind the safety of the Sinnale line. And even then, when Layla dropped her bow over her head to lie across her back, Nuala waited for Einar to ease his guard before she allowed herself to do the same.

As morning light spilled into the city streets, the exhaustion of the last few days finally took its toll. She leaned against Einar as they walked farther into safe territory. He wrapped an arm around her shoulders, keeping her close.

Soft pink sunlight colored the air and painted the bricks

and cobbles, making everything look cleaner, fresher than it would in bright sun. Nuala loved sunrise. There was a stillness, a quiet to it that usually settled her mind.

But even exhausted, even passing alive and well through her favorite time of day, a low level of tension tightened Nuala's stomach.

They'd avoided having to face the queen and reveal their fall. For now. But it loomed ahead of them. They wouldn't be able to break the bonding between them now. Nor could they hide it from the queen and king. And while she found a small sense of peace having survived the night, with Einar strong at her side, she knew they were far from done with their final fight.

CHAPTER TEN

*A*fter brief introductions to some of the Sinnale council members, including Layla's parents, Nuala and Einar were shown rooms in which to rest and bathe, and promised to be directed to the armory later that afternoon. Nuala had work to do now that she was safely within Sinnale-held territory—at the very center of their defenses. But her magic took energy and she needed rest and food first.

Though they were given separate rooms, Einar knocked on her door not long after Ulric left to get their breakfast. She'd just finished washing off the dirt, sweat and blood of the last two days, and had slipped into a clean tunic and a loose skirt.

When she let him in, he didn't say anything at first, just paced around her room. He'd taken the time to clean up as well, washing away the dried blood that had caused the council members to hesitate and back away from him when Ulric presented him. She had no doubt that all the legends of the Darkness of Glengowyn were running through their heads as they bowed to him. Einar, for his part, remained quiet, distant and respectful, never showing any emotion one way or the other.

She watched him stalk around her room and wondered if their reactions bothered him or if he preferred for people to think him that bloodthirsty and cold. He looked noble and controlled now, in clean trousers, tunic and vest. His short hair was damp, and whatever soap they'd provided for him surrounded him in a clean, earthy scent. She noticed, though, that he hadn't let down his guard in the safer surroundings. He'd strapped his sword around his waist before joining her.

Her room, small but very clean, looked smaller still with him in it. But the space was comfortable after their previous surroundings. The washbasin had been filled with fresh water. Clean, lightly scented towels were stacked under the basin stand. A blue ceramic heater in one corner was stocked with kindling, flint and wood, should she get cold. The bed was high and comfortably made up with thick blankets and several pillows. A small wooden wardrobe sat in the corner opposite the heater. Inside, she'd found several changes of clothes, all freshly laundered, some of them her own from the supply wagons that had traveled with her party from Glengowyn. The tunic and skirt she'd been able to don after bathing were her own, and having her own clothing was a comfort.

Given that the city had been at war for two years, Nuala suspected her room was one of their best and was grateful for the Sinnale's thoughtfulness.

Einar stopped pacing at the first of two large windows that spilled morning light into the room. He studied the street below, the outside walls of the building and the lock above the double panes before moving to the next window.

Checking on her security, she thought. Even here in allied territory.

"I'm sure we're safe," she commented, though she didn't stop him from doing what he thought best. He was here as her bodyguard after all. Though there was more between them—and his actions—than that. No one would begrudge him his precautions.

When he'd finished his study of the windows, he opened the wardrobe and nodded approvingly at the clothing. "I'm glad some of the wagons made it through the attack."

That had been one of his first questions to Ulric once they were inside Sinnale borders. She and Einar had both been relieved to hear the casualties of that attack had been minimal. Once she'd escaped, the fighting had ended quickly. Because of that, the supplies of arrows—both her standard; the fire-tips, which were only now being traded with the Sinnale; and Nuala's particular special arrows, also only now being allowed into Sinnale hands—had arrived safely and were waiting for her to set.

"The elves of your guard are still here," he continued. "You'll have a proper escort back to Glengowyn."

The thought of going home sent her stomach dancing with nerves. She wanted to say something about that fear, but Einar's mood seemed so pensive she decided it best to wait for him to say what he was here to say.

He finally stopped moving and settled his hands on his hips, his head bowed forward. Then he straightened. "You need rest and food. We can talk later."

"Einar..." She stopped him as he made for the door. "What's wrong?"

He held perfectly still with his back to her for a moment.

Then he turned and closed the space between them in two steps. Before she could gasp, he had her face between his palms and he was kissing her, desperately, hard, like they'd been separated again for a century. She wrapped herself around him, matching the kiss, matching the passion. She couldn't stop. Though she didn't fully understand what drove him, in that moment, she didn't care.

He lifted his mouth too soon and stared down at her. "I would do anything for you. Remember that."

She sucked in a sharp breath at the intensity in his gaze.

"I will let you go if you don't want to face banishment."

The statement startled her and she stepped back quickly as if she'd been slapped. He let her. "What are you talking about? I thought I made myself clear on this subject."

"Passion in the moment."

"How dare you?" she hissed. "After everything, how dare you presume my feelings for you are that fleeting."

"When the queen and king demanded we separate, you broke with me." He firmed his shoulders and there was no longer emotion in his expression. "You chose then."

"I chose? I knew what you would choose and simply beat you to the break."

He frowned. "You have no idea what I wanted. You never asked."

"You were the king and queen's personal guard. You have always been about duty above anything else. Your loyalty was beyond question. Of course you would choose them over me. How could I think otherwise?"

He crossed the space between them in a single step and took her shoulders in his hands, bringing his face close to hers. "Listen to this well, Nuala. I was prepared to choose banishment. I came to you that day to tell you I wanted you above everything. And *you* set *me* aside. In the name of duty."

She shook her head, denying words she couldn't believe.

"I told the queen, before I came to you, that I would not be separated from you if you wanted me. She threatened banishment, the *Or'roan*. And I chose you."

"Why didn't you tell me?" she wailed.

Two centuries. Two centuries of pain and loss and longing. Two centuries of denying this love between them. Because she *thought* he would choose his sovereigns over her.

"You made your choice."

"Only because I thought I knew what you'd say, and I didn't…" Her throat closed up as centuries of suppressed tears built and threatened to flow. "I couldn't hear you say you didn't love me enough to stay," she finally whispered. And the tears fell.

Between her exhaustion, the recent battles, the bonding with Einar, Nuala was overwhelmed and exposed. She couldn't hide from him. She couldn't control the emotions rolling through her. Regret and fear tangled with love and need, desperation and loss all one giant hand closing around her heart and squeezing.

Einar released a sigh that took all the tension from his shoulders and his grip on her arms. He hugged her close, tucking her head beneath his chin, and held her as tightly as she clung to him.

When the emotional storm started to ease, Einar skimmed one hand up and down her back, the gentle stroke a comfort.

"I've always loved you," she said. She'd held those words inside for so long, even during their initial mating, it felt cathartic to finally allow them out and hear them aloud.

"You've never told me before," he murmured into her hair.

"Neither have you," she challenged. But she knew he loved her. It was there in the *Shaerta* when they made love.

His chest rose and fell with a deep breath. "I've loved you much longer than you could know. Well before our first mating. Before the war."

She leaned back to look up at him. "Before the war? We barely spoke before then."

"I knew."

"Knew?"

"We would bond. I could feel it in my soul. If we mated, we'd bond. Our magics would mix. I knew that would... complicate things. And you would break my heart. But I couldn't stop loving you."

She wanted to cry again, but her tears had dried up. "What changed?"

"You didn't run away when you saw what I could be. You weren't afraid, after that night in the camp when the goblins snuck in. You were the only one who didn't change toward me."

"Ulric didn't. The soldiers in your regiment didn't."

"Ulric was my commander. He'd seen me in battle and knew what I was capable of. He'd already seen my worst. You don't really remember our friendship before that war, do you?"

"No."

"He was already an admired soldier from the first war. I respected him and looked up to him. I wanted to fight under his command. But until we went into battle, even I didn't know what I was capable of. He... Well, he wasn't as easy with me after that. There was respect. But no longer the camaraderie he had with the others under his command. None of the other soldiers were comfortable with me either."

He cupped her cheek in one large hand, his thumb lightly caressing her cheekbone. "But you… You worried about *me* after seeing what I became when I let myself. You came to me immediately. Washed away the blood. Checked for wounds. The same as today. You didn't shy back. You weren't afraid."

"I could never be afraid of you. Not that way."

"What way then?"

"Oh, Einar. The damage you could do to my heart terrifies me. I'm afraid of that. But I don't worry, even in the heat of battle, that you would lash out at me."

She watched his throat work as he swallowed hard. "I would do anything for you, Nuala. You know that? I would happily go into banishment, take on the *Or'roan*… I would even give you up again if that made you happier."

"Stop. Don't ever say that to me again. Not ever."

"It's not too late—"

"Enough, I said. It is too late. It was too late centuries ago. We just weren't ready to accept. I didn't trust your feelings, and you didn't trust mine. But this time… This time the bond is tightening. You can feel it too. There's no going back now. I wouldn't want to even if we could."

"Your magic?"

She looked away. "I don't know. I'll know when I try. I haven't felt different, so it's possible we haven't melded completely yet."

He stepped away from her so suddenly, she rocked backward. "I'll leave then. If we can keep the balance for a little while longer, so you can finish this last trade, maybe the king and queen will be merciful. Banishment but no curse."

She was exhausted, emotionally wrung out, and in need of food and sleep before working her magic later. He was right, it would be better if he left. If for no other reason than she'd actually sleep. But she didn't want him to go. They'd been through too much in such a short period of time. All she wanted was the comfort of his big body next to her.

"Don't," she said, flattening her hands on his chest. "Not yet. I know I need to rest, but… At least keep me company while we eat. I don't want to be alone yet."

His entire body loosened as tension dropped away and he tugged her back into his arms. "I never could refuse you anything."

She snorted, snuggling her cheek against his chest. "You refused to teach me how to fight, as I recall."

"Ah. That was an order from King Varim. He didn't think you'd need it and was afraid it would take too much time away from working your magic."

"Ulric and Althir still taught me to throw a knife."

"Ulric is a favorite of the sovereigns. He could get away with more than I could. At least where you were concerned. And Althir…Althir could charm his way out of a *dargem* pit."

She shivered at the mention of the deadly creatures that called the Unseen Plain their home. They were the stuff of elven nightmares, grotesque and lethal. Since she didn't want to have nightmares when she finally slept, she concentrated on the first part of his comment.

"You're a favorite with the sovereigns too. Queen Rohannah made that clear when she ordered me to stay away from you. She didn't want to lose you any more than she wanted to endanger my magic."

"I'm...a good threat. Having me behind them ensures no one risks their wrath."

Nuala pursed her lips. "Hmm. I'm not sure that's the only reason the queen favors you."

She felt his silent chuckle in the sudden movement of his chest against her cheek. Looking up, she scowled. "Why are you laughing?"

"I'm surprised. Is that jealousy I hear?"

Her scowl deepened. "Don't you dare tease me. The queen is beautiful and powerful, and she gets what she wants. And you're always around her. How could she not want you?"

He leaned down and kissed her frowning mouth, the humor in his eyes mixing with tenderness.

"As I've said, my heart has been yours for a very long time now. Even the queen couldn't change that." He set his nose close to hers, forcing her to look him in the eyes. "And she never tried. She recognized a lost cause when she saw one."

Wrinkling her nose, trying to ignore the heat in her cheeks, she shrugged. "Fine."

"And you?"

"Me what?"

"There have been men since me who've wanted you. Powerful elves."

"Oh, I was never one to worry about. After the war, the queen and king made it perfectly clear to all that I was off limits. Too valuable to risk." She couldn't stop herself from sneering that last. Her *value* had kept her from the man she loved for so long, resentment was a ready companion.

"So…" Einar drawled, tilting his head to the side. "There would have been others, if not for their order?"

She raised her brows at the sudden deepening of his voice. Her turn to smile. "You know better than that."

"Do I?"

"You should by now." She snuggled close to him, running her hands over his shoulders and down his chest, loving the feel of his heartbeat picking up under her palms. "I only ever wanted you. I still want you. More than I want food or sleep."

She rose onto her toes and kissed him, hard, sure. Letting him know just how much she did want him. Silly man, thinking she could ever bed another after being with him. He hesitated to return her kiss, and she knew why. But she took his pause as a challenge rather than a warning. She nibbled her way along his jaw, then kissed the strong column of his throat, licking her way across freshly cleaned skin.

"Nuala…"

His groan made her smile. She slid her hands up under his shirt, flattening her palms on the solid muscles of his lower abdomen. Low enough to hint and tease, promising without delivering. Yet.

He gripped her wrists but didn't do more, and she knew he would give in. He could no more resist her than she could him. There was power in that knowledge, power magnified by her love for him. She continued to kiss her way down his throat, to the hollow at the base of his neck. His shirt was in the way, so she nuzzled it aside, leaving her hands braced exactly where they were. His muscles were tight everywhere now, and the tension in his grip was thrilling.

"The food will be here soon," he said, his voice very deep.

"Yes," she agreed without stopping her exploration of him with her mouth.

She let her fingernails dig ever so slightly into his skin, and his body jerked in response. Releasing her wrists, he shifted his hands to her ass and pulled her tight to his erection.

"This should stop," he muttered, but his fingers kneaded her flesh and he ground his hips against hers, belying his words.

"Are you sure you want me to stop?" she said into his neck, before biting down lightly on the skin between his throat and shoulder.

"Goddess, no."

The sheer desperation in his voice made her chuckle. "Then I think I'll continue."

Finally moving her hands from where they were trapped between their bodies, she slipped her palms higher, caressing his skin softly with her nails. The movement pushed his shirt higher, giving her access to all the hard planes of muscle. She dropped to her knees in front of him, despite his warning growl and his attempt to keep her in place. The heat of his skin was a lure she refused to resist. Placing her lips gently on his abdomen, she reveled in the trembling of muscle she felt.

She trailed her tongue down the center of his stomach, stopping only when she reached the top of his trousers. Then she pushed the material down ever so slightly and licked.

The sound he made in response was part moan, part shout, but muffled as if he didn't want to make too much noise. The response pleased her. She nuzzled her cheek against his erection, still unfortunately confined by his trousers.

"This can't be very comfortable. Wouldn't you be happier

without these?" She tugged gently at the top of his trousers to make her point.

"Yes."

The gravel of his voice sent a spike of heat to her core. But before she could make good on removing his trousers, someone knocked at the door. With a soft grunt of regret, she nuzzled his erection again, then stood.

Grinning, she pointed to the bed. "Maybe you should sit down and make that beautifully hard cock less obvious. We wouldn't want to scare anyone."

His dark expression only made her grin more.

When he was seated, uncomfortably, on the edge of the mattress, she opened the door and let in a human woman carrying a large tray. She startled when she saw Einar in the room.

"Oh, I'm sorry, my lord. I left your meal in your room. Will I bring it here?"

He nodded, quick and sharp, without unclenching his jaw.

Setting her tray down on the small table next to the bed, the woman hurried off, glancing nervously at the large warrior elf scowling from his place on the bed.

When she was gone, Nuala said, "You're scaring her, you know. You might want to try a less…threatening expression."

He snorted but still didn't speak. When the girl returned, she looked around for a place to put the second tray, her gaze continuing to jump nervously toward Einar.

"Here," Nuala said, feeling sorry for the poor woman. She took the tray. "Don't let him scare you. He's just…in a mood."

The woman tried to smile, but when she glanced at Einar again, her faint smile dropped. "If there will be nothing else?"

"No. Thank you very much for the food."

The human dipped into a slight curtsy and fled, closing the door solidly behind her.

"Einar. That wasn't very nice."

She turned to scold him and found him standing in front of her. Silently, he took the tray, set it to one side on the floor, and yanked her back into his arms.

"You want nice," he said in that same gravelly voice. "I'll give you nice."

His threat sent a shiver of excitement across her skin, and she sank against him as he finally captured her mouth in a hard, demanding kiss.

CHAPTER ELEVEN

*N*uala barely had time to catch her breath before Einar had her stripped naked and sprawled across the bed. The *Shaerta* roared through her, making her skin so sensitive, his every touch was an exquisite balance between pleasure and pain. Before she could gain the upper hand again, he settled between her legs and licked into her wet, hot folds, sending her body into a spiral of desperation.

Knowing there were other people in the building, near enough to hear her, she kept her screams of pleasure locked behind clenched teeth. Then Einar's revenge swept her up into a fast, hard orgasm so overwhelming it stole her voice.

He tried to take advantage of her loss of control, to keep her in the throes of his revenge. But she wanted too much from him to allow that. Despite his superior size, she surprised him by flipping him onto his back. Her needs rode her hard, making her rough as she opened his belt and wrenched his trousers apart, forcing them down his hips. She didn't even bother to fully strip him, just leaned over his throbbing cock and took him into her mouth.

Einar's back arched off the bed and he dropped his hands to her head, burying his fingers in the thick mass of her hair. The long locks fell in waves around her, covering his hips, creating a curtain that added intimacy as she licked and sucked him.

Controlling his body, this warrior so feared by everyone else, gave her as much pleasure as his mouth had just given her. She couldn't stop, even when she knew he was close to losing control. And she didn't want to. His pants and moans, the near painful grip of his hands, sent her own body tightening again, climbing toward another orgasm without him even having to touch her.

His scent rose up to surround her, mixing with the already potent *Shaerta* to drive her beyond thought. Pleasure, need, taking and giving. Nothing else mattered in that moment. Only the hard length of him between her lips, the desperate sounds he made from between clenched teeth, the rasps of their panting mingling in the quiet room.

Driven beyond madness by her desires, she straddled one of his legs and rubbed herself along the smooth leather of his trousers, even as she continued to savor the taste of his cock. The sensation of cool, smooth material against her hot, wet clit pushed her to the very edge of her control. And when she felt Einar pulse in her mouth, when he ground out her name and came with a suppressed roar, she followed. The spiraling pleasure jerked through her body as she continued to suck the last of Einar's orgasm from him.

Panting and gloriously, if momentarily, satisfied, Nuala released him from her lips and nuzzled his hip with her cheek.

His eyes were so dark they were nearly black, and the love and desire there squeezed around her heart. He still had one hand in her hair, caressing her scalp gently, and she wanted to purr like one of the cats she remembered from her last visit to Sinnale.

"You'll eat now," he growled down at her, his voice so harsh another might have thought him angry.

She raised her brows and smiled, glancing at his semi-erect cock.

"The food," he clarified. And she laughed.

"You'll eat—the food—too. It's been a long night. Then I do need to sleep. But—" she held up a hand when he started to speak, "—I want you to stay with me, sleep here with me."

He still looked like he wanted to protest. "The bonding… we made things worse just now."

"And I want you here too much to care if we continue to make things worse." She crawled up his body and settled beside him, leaning over to hold his gaze so he couldn't doubt her words. "It's too late, Einar. And I don't care. For you, for us, I will take the worst punishment the queen and king will hand out."

"You're not scared of the *Or'roan*?"

"Oh, I'm scared of that. I don't want to meet a permanent end to my soul. Mostly because it means I'll only have this lifetime with you. And I want more. I don't want to risk your afterlife, your lifetimes either. If you walked away from me to avoid the *Or'roan*, I'd let you go."

"Never," he hissed, his arms tightening around her hard and fast.

She released a little breath, only just then realizing a small part of her had worried he'd make the choice to abandon what they had if she offered him the out.

"Then you should know I will always choose this life with you," she said, "no matter how long we have, whether we can travel into the next realm together or not. I can't continue without you anymore. I don't want to."

"I don't want to either." He kissed her, a soft promise. When he straightened, though, his brow was creased and his mouth tightened. "I can feel a difference," he said quietly. "In my magic. Already I can feel a difference."

She let her attention turn inward, toward that place at her very center where her essence and magic mixed to make her who she was. She concentrated on the swirls of energy, the ebbs and flows. And realized she too felt different.

There were changes happening. She wouldn't be able to tell how those changes would manifest in her magic until she tried to work it. But she and Einar were linked now, their bonding almost fully complete. And with that came a melding of powers and talents, leaving in its wake something new and untried.

She refocused on him. "As I said. Too late. So now there's no reason for you to leave. Stay with me. I'll sleep better knowing you're next to me."

He kissed her again before saying, "I don't want to be anywhere else ever again."

Ulric and Layla came personally to show Nuala to the armory and the room set up for her work. Einar insisted on escorting her despite the fact that she was safe with her cousin.

She allowed Einar and Layla, busy discussing the tensile strength of the steel used in various elf swords, to move ahead so she could have a private word with Ulric as they walked.

"Your brother?" she said in their own language, in case Ulric didn't want his feelings on the subject known to the Sinnale.

The expression on Ulric's face was not friendly. His blue eyes narrowed and a set of deep lines furrowed his brow. "The humans have agreed to hold Althir in a comfortable prison for the time being. I think they give him too much luxury."

"He is your brother."

"His selfishness almost got Layla killed. *He* almost killed Layla. Though he claims he didn't know it was her when he fired." This last he muttered quietly, reluctantly, as if part of him believed Althir and resented doing so.

"Ah." She understood, better than Ulric knew. The brothers had never been particularly close, so Althir having anything to do with harming the woman Ulric loved would likely override his brotherly feelings. The fact that Althir could have killed Layla, whether he meant to or not... Nuala wasn't particularly surprised Ulric was so angry. She could imagine the feeling too well when it came to Einar. Still...

Ulric and Althir's relationship was unique. Most elf siblings weren't born so close together—they were usually separated by centuries rather than decades like her cousins. She'd always thought it a shame they couldn't get along better. They were much more alike than either would care to admit.

Not the least being their loyalty to the king and queen. She often thought Althir's jealousy of Ulric came from that loyalty and the favor the sovereigns paid the older brother. And while his turning traitor had shocked her deeply, a part of her wondered if Althir had done that because the sovereigns didn't acknowledge him the way they did Ulric.

"But he's helping the humans now," she said. "You begrudge him some comfort? He's provided information that will eventually help end the war."

Ulric didn't answer for several minutes. She'd decided he wouldn't when he finally said, "I can't trust him ever again. I would have killed him for the threat he was to Layla. There's been too much damage between us for me to think kindly on Althir."

She sighed. A shame, but not unexpected. "Should I... Should I visit him while I'm here?"

"He's not allowed visitors from Glengowyn yet. On order of the king and queen. They worry he'll...corrupt other elves. His charm..."

Althir's magics were tied up in his charm, and he could be very persuasive if he chose to be. Some in Glengowyn whispered Althir was the first to defect, the one who lured the other traitors to the Sorcerers. She had her doubts about that rumor, but it made the sovereigns' order regarding visitors reasonable.

"You visit him, though?" she asked.

"I don't. But not because of the order."

"Then why?"

"I'm still tempted to kill him."

"I had to kill an elf." She blurted the sentence before she realized she would. "One of the traitors who helped in the attack on the caravan. I... I'm not sure I would have if you hadn't confirmed that I could."

"I'm sorry." He sighed. "Maybe I shouldn't have told you."

"No. That's not what I mean. He would have handed me over to the Sorcerers. To be used and drained and eventually killed. I don't regret killing him. In fact, I felt very little about having done it. I wouldn't have known it possible without you, though, and so I might not have tried. You helped save my life by telling me." She shrugged and glanced at him from the corner of her eye. "I guess I'm trying to say thank you for being honest with me."

"Always, cousin. Always." He walked beside her a few more paces before saying, very softly, "I will hate to see you banished."

She pursed her lips. "It's obvious now?"

"That you've bonded with Einar? Yes. They won't be happy when they find out."

"I know. We're prepared."

"I wish I could save you from that as well."

She gave him a small, sad smile. "No one could. But we'll be okay."

"This will affect the magics for the arrows."

He wasn't asking. He knew as well as she did that it would. "I'll keep you aware of what happens. I won't endanger the Sinnale with inadequate weaponry."

He took her hand and squeezed, a gesture that said more than his words could.

"You've lost a brother and a cousin in a war never meant for us," she said quietly.

"I didn't lose my cousin to the war. I lost her to love. And I can't fault her that." He met her gaze. "I am happy for you.

You and Einar…you share something deep. I haven't seen you this content in centuries. And that, at least, pleases me."

This time her smile was genuine and big. "Thank you."

They reached the armory then and switched back to speaking in the Sinnale language for Layla's sake.

She held open a thick wooden door for them, gesturing them into a large room filled with strung bows, swords of various sizes, a few vests of chainmail and helmets, a plethora of knives ranging from daggers to throwing darts, a pile of what Nuala guessed were the makings for explosives, and racks of elf arrows—both the regular arrows typically traded with the Sinnale, and the fire-tips which were only now being allowed into Sinnale hands.

The fire-tips had arrowheads that burned as hot as lava after their release, deadly and dangerous. While they could slice through most barriers, including magical ones, they could also ignite major fires if not used carefully. Until recently, the king and queen hadn't wanted that power in the hands of their neighbors.

Several elves created the fire-tips so Nuala was rarely tasked to make many. The king and queen had her concentrate on ordinary arrows—hers were some of the best and so traded well with the Sinnale before the war—and making her special arrows.

The material for which currently sat at the center of the room. A large stack of the pre-fletched, hollowed shafts waited for her to finish them. Several boxes of additional material were piled next to the stack—shrapnel to fill the shafts, arrowheads and leather wraps specifically designed for her specialty.

Without her magic, her spell to set the arrows, they would

never fly. Too heavy and off balance when filled with small sharp shards of metal, the arrows should have been useless. But once set with her spell, they became a dangerous bomb, exploding and unleashing chaos wherever they landed. These arrows had helped her people win the last goblin war. The Sinnale were counting on them to put an end to their own war.

If she could get them to work now that her magic had mixed with Einar's.

"Do you have everything you need?" Layla asked as Nuala studied her work area.

There was a comfortable-looking bench for her to sit at, all the tools she needed to hand. And a small, empty table to one side of the bench.

"Everything looks good. The table?"

"For water, meals. Whatever you might need."

"She won't eat while working," Einar said. "But make sure there's water for her."

Layla left to get the water. Nuala stared at Einar for several moments, knowing he was thinking the same thing she was—could she do what was necessary anymore? Could she work the spell, the special magic only she'd ever been able to wield, and turn these arrows into bombs?

Ulric clapped Einar on the back of the shoulder, breaking into their silence. "Come. We'll leave my cousin to her work and you and I can discuss some security issues."

Though he went reluctantly, Einar allowed Ulric to lead him out. A moment later, a pitcher of fresh water and a glass were delivered and left on the table. Then Nuala was alone.

CHAPTER TWELVE

$\mathscr{N}$uala stared at the hollowed-out arrow shafts, and for the first time since discovering this spell, knew real trepidation. She settled herself on the bench, took up the first hollow shaft and dropped in some shrapnel, filling it completely from the closed base where it had already been properly fletched, all the way to the tip where she inserted the point.

As she wrapped securing leather around the arrowhead, she closed her eyes and began the spell, sending power through her body, molding it into the song of enchantment and death that was the weapon. A quiet, mumbling swing of words fell from her lips to swirl around the arrow, infusing and setting it.

But as she worked, the song felt…different. A word, here or there, came out wrong and yet fit perfectly into what she was singing. The tone of certain notes changed, by a flat or sharp, a whole octave deeper or higher. Yet the rhythm felt powerful, the pour of magic through her body flowed easily. It didn't fight the changes in the spell. In fact, the new twists of magic she accessed grew stronger as she chanted, hinting at the final shape without revealing it, bringing a certainty of purpose and strength both different and familiar.

She could almost feel the influence of Einar's magic mingling with her own, turning into its own creation. That it mixed so easily, so well, so perfectly was both surprising and somehow expected. Yet, even as she sang, as she formed the spell and poured power into it, she had no idea what she was really creating. Still a weapon. Maybe even more powerful than her previous spell. But with a difference she couldn't understand. Something more…personal. Something more precise…

When her music faded and she returned from the sensory realms of working the magic back to a more physical state, she stared down at the finished arrow in her hands. A faint golden glow faded as she watched. And then the arrow looked like any other.

What had she done? What would this new creation do?

She set the enigma aside, selected a second arrow shaft and attempted to set it with the original spell. This time, her power flowed in the old ways, lacking the changeable influence of Einar's magic. And when she was done, she'd created one of the original weapons she was here to set. Again she went to the arrow shafts, again the magic bowed to the original intention of the spell. But after another five arrows, the magic bent again. And Nuala made another of the strange anomalous arrows.

Late into the night she worked, remembering to drink only

when she felt faint. Her body faded away with each spell-casting, so that she only noticed discomfort for brief minutes between the magics. In those moments, she felt the growing exhaustion that would eventually force her to stop and sleep. But she ignored both the physical and magical depletion to continue working.

When she could no longer concentrate enough to properly form either of the spells, she took stock of her work.

To one side lay almost a hundred of the new type of arrows. To the other, three times that many of her originally spelled weapons. She let out a breath and selected one of the new, studying it, feeling the magic within. She closed her eyes and opened her sense, trying to discern how the new arrow might work, but the solution eluded her. With her original arrows, she'd known as she made them what they would become. This time, the outcome was a mystery.

How could she give these to the Sinnale when she didn't even know what they did? Would they even fly with all the shrapnel inside them, given the changes in the spell? So many uncertainties. And no opportunity to test any possible theory. The human council expected what they'd ordered, what they'd fairly traded for.

Now what?

She set the arrow back in its pile and gulped down the remaining water, not surprised to find her throat so dry it had tightened up. She moved to the cot Layla had provided in one dark corner of the room, curled onto her side, and was asleep instantly.

Though there were windows in the room, she found it impossible to tell how long she'd slept after she returned to consciousness. It was still dark out, so she could have slept for a quarter hour, several hours, even a full day into the next night. Sitting up, she noticed a basin of clean washing water had been brought into the room. The water pitcher was filled again. And there was a small plate of cheese and nuts on the table beside the water.

The idea of food made her stomach roll in disgust, but the water sounded like joy. Once she'd sated her thirst, took care of bodily functions, and paced a few times around the room to loosen up muscles, she returned to setting arrows.

When exhaustion took her again, it was full sunlight, though she still wasn't sure what time. No timer chimes sounded through the city. No time device of any kind was left in the large room. As she worked, time lost meaning anyway, and she stopped only long enough to nap again, then returned to the arrows.

The sun was down, the room shadowed in the corners where the light from the hanging gaslamp refused to go, by the time she'd worked her way through most of the empty arrow shafts.

Einar quietly entered the room sometime during her working. But he remained as unobtrusive and invisible as only a well-trained bodyguard could. Even Nuala only barely noted his presence, and she was overly aware of him.

She let the last song fade away and placed the arrow she'd been working on the pile with the new arrows. The two piles had remained a three-to-one ratio of traditional to new. And she still had no idea what the newest arrows did.

The rest of the water in the pitcher wetted her dry throat before she finally turned to face Einar.

He didn't even have to question her aloud. She could see his concern and curiosity in the slight raise of his brows.

"These—" she pointed to the larger of the two piles, "—are the arrows I'm here to produce. These others are new."

"What do the new ones do?"

"I have no idea," she admitted. "They're different, a product of our melding. But... I have no idea what they're capable of."

He stared at the smaller pile. "What will you tell Ulric, the human council?"

She stood and stretched, letting her spine pop as she worked out the kinks of sitting for so long. "Ulric... Ulric knows we've bonded. He can sense the change."

Einar nodded.

"I'm hoping to persuade him to let me test one or two of these before allowing the humans to use any of them. I don't want to be responsible for any Sinnale deaths because the weapon backfires."

"Reasonable. And you've managed to produce the arrows they traded for—at least a good number of them came out correctly. That bodes well."

"Maybe." Though she wasn't sure what to make of this mixing of abilities from one moment to the next. "I hope it will be enough to satisfy them until we can figure out what these others do."

"Ulric will make sure it is. Now, you need food."

She blinked. Her mind had been on the rhythm and words of the new spell as she tried to analyze them for a possible explanation. Einar's reminder that she needed to eat made her stomach growl.

"I guess I do need food." She chuckled and left the arrows to join him in his position next to the door. "How long have you been keeping vigil there?"

"Inside the room? Not long. I didn't want to distract you."

His expression remained neutral, but she didn't miss his careful phrasing. "Inside the room not long. How long did you watch over me from outside the room?"

"I've been here all along. I couldn't leave you alone and vulnerable in a strange place. Even if we are surrounded by allies."

He spoke as if she should have known better and her question baffled him. She should have known better. How else would Einar think?

"Come, Ulric has food prepared and waiting in a more comfortable setting."

Without touching her, he led her back down the corridor. The lack of physical contact was exactly what she needed. After working so much magic, her skin was always overly sensitive, and a simple touch often hurt. Einar had always understood this, better than anyone else.

As she thought back on their years of friendship and loving, she realized he always did what was right and best for her—or at least what he thought was best.

The room he led her to was small but comfortably set with a long table and benches. The table itself was covered with more cheese, dried fruits and some fresh bread.

Layla looked up from setting out plates and greeted them with a smile. "I hope it will be enough. The war has been difficult on our food stores, but we've been doing better lately.

We don't have much fresh meat, but there is some dried meat available if you require it."

Nuala waved that off. "I don't need meat. And simple foods are best."

They settled around the table and everyone quietly filled a plate. Einar watched her take her first few bites before taking any himself.

"I'm sorry there's no wine," Layla said into the silence. "There's very little left in the city. And it will be several years before we can start producing again."

"Water is better for me now." Nuala sighed. "But I will miss Sinnale wine. I have for the last few years. Your grapes always seem to produce more interesting flavors than ours."

Layla smiled. "One of the things my parents got the best use out of when trading for weapons. Sinnale wine."

She stared at Nuala for several moments and Nuala held her gaze, wondering at the considering look. She was used to a distant kind of reverence from her own people. And in years past, humans had dealt with her with a kind of awe. But many humans approached the Glengowyn elves that way. She was one of many to them, not considered unique the way she was among her own people.

Now, though, Layla and a handful of other humans knew she was special. Different. She had a feeling she was about to find out how that knowledge would affect their attitudes toward her going forward.

Layla's question, when she finally spoke, surprised Nuala, however.

"Why did you have to come here? That was never made clear in the negotiations with the queen. And despite being willing to trade your special arrows with us to help end the war, she was vague when it came to you."

Nuala shrugged and swallowed her food. "The queen and king are both very protective of me."

"Yes. Which is why I'm surprised they would send you into a war zone."

"Oh, this isn't the first time I've been in a war zone. I developed these arrows for the second goblin war."

"They helped us end that war relatively quickly," Ulric added.

"Not quickly enough," she said, looking at her cousin.

He held her gaze, his expression full of understanding. No one who'd been part of those battles had escaped without scars.

"But to answer your question…" She faced Layla again. "I have to…set the arrows close to the point at which they'll be used. They travel in quivers fine over short distances and so long as there aren't too many in a single quiver. They can be packed with our other spelled arrows for even more secure travel—though I would recommend keeping the fire-tips and my arrows separate. But they can't be stacked in large numbers and carted over long distances, already assembled and spelled. The movement, time and quantity together triggers the spell."

"They explode without being fired," Ulric said. "We learned that the hard way."

Nuala glanced down at her plate. That was one of her scars from the war, a mistake that had cost several strong warrior elves their lives. Einar shifted minutely closer to her, still not touching—not enough time had elapsed for her skin and nerves to have settled—but enough to make his comforting presence felt. She released the tension with a breath and looked up.

"After the…accident. We knew the arrows had to be transported in individual parts, and I'd have to be camped near the battles to be able to set them."

"So, you went into the war," Layla said.

"I went into the war." Nuala blinked back more memories. "And after, the queen in particular but both the sovereigns knew that not only were these weapons something too dangerous to share with outsiders, they were too unstable to trade easily. They also never wanted to risk me being kidnapped or held captive by someone we traded with after I was sent in to set the arrows."

"That's why Nuala hasn't come into Sinnale in a century," Ulric said. "Their protectiveness of her has gotten worse over the years."

Einar grunted, a surprising sound that drew all their gazes. He didn't look up from his plate, just ignored their attention, so they returned to their conversation.

"So," Layla said, "once the traitor elves defected and it became clear this war was coming to Glengowyn if they did nothing, like it or not, they decided to risk you by trading these arrows with us."

"In their way." She dipped her head toward Einar. "They sent me with their most feared personal bodyguard. They did try to minimize the risk."

"The traitors knew who you were though. They guessed you'd come eventually."

Einar grunted again. This time he did speak. "They were likely watching for her, keeping at least one or two of the traitors with each group of minions sent to attack the caravans."

Nuala pursed her lips. "There was no way around my coming here. For your people to have these arrows, to end this war faster, it was necessary for me to come."

"I'm glad they allowed it," Layla said. "We're stronger now, with the reintroduction of the elven weaponry. But the war is dragging on. The Sorcerers continue to capture our people and use them or turn them into minions. We need to drive them out."

"The information Althir provides?"

"Very helpful. We've been able to engage them beyond their own border for the first time since the border was set. We know where their vulnerable spots are, even the location of their individual strongholds outside the main citadel, all the places we'll have to destroy to drive them out. But we haven't been able to break through their defenses thoroughly enough to move far enough into their territory to end things."

Nuala caught Ulric's gaze as she said, "Some of the arrows...didn't turn out as they should have. It happens sometimes." She lied and made sure Ulric knew it. "I'll need to run a few tests on the different ones before they're allowed into a battle. In the meantime, the ones provided combined with our ordinary arrows and the fire-tips should be sufficient to aid in an offensive."

Ulric nodded in understanding, his gaze darting to Einar and then to Layla. Layla didn't comment but her eyes narrowed.

She was smart, Ulric's mate. She knew something wasn't exactly right with what Nuala had said, but she kept that knowledge to herself and outwardly accepted the story.

"I'll be sure the arms marshal knows which arrows are not ready to be used," she said.

Nuala felt tension she'd only barely been aware of uncurl. Until she could figure out what the new arrows did, she did not want to risk another accident. She'd never forgive herself if some of the Sinnale were killed because of her, the way her own people had died before she knew more about her shrapnel arrows. She would not make that mistake again.

CHAPTER THIRTEEN

The Sinnale had already started planning another offensive before Nuala and her arrows entered the city, with the new weapons at the core of their plans. Once Nuala and Einar had arrived, the human council finalized their strategy and began organizing their people.

Nuala spent the next day and a half in the armory. While trying to unravel the purpose of the new arrows, she also ensured they weren't inadvertently added to the weaponry the humans planned to use for the coming battle. Unfortunately, the ultimate results of the spell continued to elude her.

"This has never happened before," she complained to Einar after the first day. "How can I not know what magic I've wrought?"

"You've never dealt with blended magics before," he assured her, remaining a calming presence beside her the entire time. "You'll understand soon."

But when another half day passed with her at a loss, Einar insisted she leave the armory to rest. "Ulric will make sure none of these make it into the battle preparations. You won't find answers if you're too exhausted to think."

She didn't want to stop but knew he was right. If she didn't sleep properly, she might even miss the answer right in front of her.

They hadn't had much time alone since she started her work in the armory. Between the exertions of her magic and the time spent trying to unravel the spell she'd placed on the new arrows, she'd never stopped to wonder how their bonding had affected his magic. Or him.

Without argument or even the need for words, he followed her into her room. As soon as she shut the door, he gathered her close and kissed her. The kiss was gentle, not demanding, but she felt his longing in the tightness of his muscles. She sighed into the sensations and gave herself over to his kiss, returning it with equal tenderness.

"I've missed this," he murmured. "Only a few days, and I've missed kissing you. I won't be able to go back to how things were between us."

"Me neither." She eased back enough to look at him directly. "I have no intention of going back, either. But…"

He stiffened. "But?"

"We haven't stopped to consider how this has affected your magic. Until now, everyone's been more concerned with what might happen to my skills. I haven't stopped to think what this might have done to you."

Holding her at his side, he led her to the bed. "I haven't attempted anything yet."

They lay down, fully clothed, and she rested her head on his chest. "Is your…is your battle state part of your magic?" No one knew, at least not that she'd ever spoken with, though she was sure the queen knew, and no one seemed inclined to ask him. She'd never been brave enough to bring up the topic.

He remained silent for a while, and she gave him time, listening to his heart beat steady against her cheek.

Finally, he said, "I've never been sure. I don't feel like I'm tapping magic when I…let go. Unlike the owls. I feel that, the mixing of magic and my essence to make that possible. In battle… All I ever feel is rage. And when I turn the rage loose, I become the Darkness."

"So you'll still be capable of doing what you do in battle?" She realized that gave her a measure of relief she hadn't anticipated. She was quite certain one of the things that kept Einar safe was the fear he inspired. Even the king wouldn't think to challenge him in combat. But if that had changed because of what they'd done, he would be vulnerable.

"That skill at least should be fine," he reassured. "The owls…"

"Has something changed with that?"

"Not that I can put words to. I can still feel the ability to speak with them within me. But something in the calling has changed."

"The calling? Being able to get them to come to you?"

"It hasn't gone away. I can call them. I think. But there's a difference to it. I can't really explain. Maybe a different focus?"

"Different focus. That sort of describes what I'm sensing in the new arrows. No. Not difference so much as *more* focus. There's something…precise about the spell, something specific that wasn't there before."

"Yes. That's a good way to explain it. There's a precision

to the feel of the calling now, a specificity that wasn't required before."

"Does it make things more difficult?"

She felt his shrug. "I haven't tried to actually bring an owl to me yet, so I can't say. I'm going on the way the magic feels."

"You should try. Soon."

"It isn't as important as the new arrows. It can wait."

She licked her lips before asking, "Will they stop carrying messages for Glengowyn if you're banished?"

"I don't know that either. When the king first threatened me with banishment if I didn't stay away from you, I asked the owls and they said they wouldn't continue. But…a lot of time has passed since then. And with the change in my magic… I'll have to ask them again."

She didn't think the threat of losing the owls would be enough to earn them forgiveness from their sovereigns, but it was something to consider.

Her head lifted slightly as Einar pulled in a deep breath. "Sleep, Nuala. We can worry about these things another time."

He was right. They would worry about them when they returned to Glengowyn. A small part of her wondered if they should bother going back. Just take themselves into banishment now before the king and queen publicly sent them away. It wouldn't save them from the consequences of their actions. And the sovereigns, if they wanted to, could place the *Or'roan* on her and Einar no matter where they went. But it would be easier not to have to face the censure of the king or the wrath of the queen in person.

She closed her eyes and allowed her tired body the rest it

needed, taking comfort in the fact that at least she and Einar would face that future together, no matter what the sovereigns decided.

Nuala watched the final preparations for the offensive strike against the Sorcerers' borders from the rooftop of the council's meeting hall. Gaslamps lit the movements of humans in and out of the hall and through the neighboring streets. A cool breeze ruffled the night, bringing a freshness to the air along with the anticipation of a battle to come.

She'd spent more time with her new arrows, digging through the layers of the spell. And had come to one conclusion.

"They have to be tried," she said to Einar, who stood at her back. "I have to use one to see what it will do."

He didn't pretend not to understand her meaning. "You're not a soldier. You're too valuable to be sent directly into a battle like this. I will go and try the weapon."

"No." She turned and faced him. "It's my spell. My risk. And you won't *know* the difference the way I will when I use one. There's no other place to try them. I can't just fire one randomly at a target like the others. There's...something about that sort of experiment that feels more dangerous than firing one in battle." She raised her hands, palms up. "I wish I could explain better."

"Nuala, I can't allow you to go into this fight. You're not prepared."

"I've been fighting since we left Glengowyn."

"This isn't your war. It's the Sinnale's. Besides, the king and queen—"

"Are about to impose severe punishments on us for our love. They will hardly blame you more if you take me into a fight." She stepped close and cupped his cheeks. His jaw was hard as stone beneath her palms, and he refused to meet her gaze when she looked up at him.

"Einar. This is the only way to test them. I don't dare leave them untested. I can't move them now that they've been set. They're more dangerous like this, so I can't just walk away and relinquish the responsibility of them to the humans. I *have* to solve this. And it has to be done in battle where the only ones hurt will be the enemy."

"I don't want you to do this."

The petulance in his voice forced a half laugh from her. "I don't want to either. I'm more than aware of my deficiencies in a fight. But I'll stay back from the ground attack, in the rooftops with the other archers."

"That position is not safe from the Sorcerers' spells."

"Safer than being in the middle of swinging swords."

"Not by much."

"You know this has to be done." She rubbed her thumbs across his cheeks, trying to loosen the tight muscles under her fingers.

"I don't like it. So you will follow my direction. I will be by your side every moment."

"I expected nothing less."

"And if I say run, fall back or give you any other warning to leave the field, you will go."

She nodded. "I'm not trying to get myself killed. I just don't want any of our allies killed either." She licked her lips. "And a concession from you."

His brows rose sharply as he dropped his chin back. "A concession from me? I'm the warrior between us."

"Yes and that's the problem. We'll be in the middle of a conflict that isn't yours any more than it's mine. It's for the Sinnale to drive the Sorcerers out. We do our part with weapons. But we're not here to really fight. I don't want you in the middle of things. And I will make it clear to Ulric that you are not taking part as anything but my bodyguard. I'm not taking part except to discover what these new arrows really do in the only way that won't endanger the humans. But beyond that, no. You are not here to be their Darkness."

The night breeze blew through his short hair, rippling the edges around his ears so the points were more prominent than usual. Light from the gaslamps below bathed his features but kept his eyes dark and difficult to read. She didn't flinch away from his silent look, though. He had to understand, his safety was as important to her as hers was to him.

"You are the only one I will be the Darkness for ever again," he said quietly. "My loyalty is with you now. Not Glengowyn. And if you ask me to fight, I will. If you ask me to avoid fighting—except where I must defend you—I will. From this time forward, you're my city, my people, my life."

Her chest ached at the declaration, making it impossible to speak. So she did what she wanted to do anyway. She drew his face close to hers and kissed him, letting just a hint of the *Shaerta* rise to add weight and power to their kiss. Letting him understand she felt exactly the same way.

She only stopped to avoid getting carried away, but she rested her head against his forehead for a long moment. Then she said, "Let's go talk with Ulric."

CHAPTER FOURTEEN

uala watched from a rooftop as the madness of battle raged below in the streets. Minions and Sinnale fought just inside the Sorcerers' border, swords clashing, the sounds of screams, metal on metal, shouts and the *thwack* of launching arrows matched only by the roar of magic.

The Sorcerers remained behind the main front but made themselves known in the drop of fire spells, which melted cobbles and brick and any hapless living thing that got in their way. Bolts of energy slammed into the midst of the chaos along with the fire, creating a cacophony of death. The Sinnale archers focused their efforts on the Sorcerers, making the attacks less consistent and overwhelming than they might have been otherwise.

Nuala even witnessed the death of one Sorcerer who happened to be standing too near when an archer finally used one of her special arrows. The shrapnel carried a spell of its own that punched through magic shields. The Sorcerer in the way of that shrapnel died in bloody shreds.

A cheer rose from the surrounding archers, spurring the Sinnale attack below.

After that, the attacking spells from the Sorcerers were even more sporadic, the focus almost defensive. The archers kept their attention on the rooftops, protecting the street soldiers below. Now that her weapons had been tried successfully, others used them as well, carefully but with a kind of relish that was almost disturbing. If Nuala hadn't known exactly what these people had been through over the last two years, she might have been bothered by their glee.

As the fighting moved deeper into the Sorcerers' territory, Nuala and the other archers followed. Einar, true to his word, stayed with her and out of the mêlée below. She kept her distance from the fighting too, remaining to the rear of the archers as they descended to street level to find another rooftop vantage point.

Down on the ground, she felt infinitely more vulnerable and so stayed close to Einar. Unlike their entrance into the city, however, no one was after them specifically this time and that made their passage somehow easier.

At the next rooftop, Nuala got her opportunity to try her new arrow. She'd only brought three with her, with the intention of using only one. And while she carried more ordinary-spelled arrows in her quiver, they were only to defend herself if it became necessary. To Einar's surprise and approval, she'd also strapped his knife to her hip. Though she had no intention of getting involved in the fighting, battles changed directions fast and there were some situations in which a bow was less useful than a knife.

She spotted the Sorcerer as she rose just above a low parapet to study the street. Nuala had taken a position away from the others, putting herself beyond the focus of most of the Sinnale archers. None of them paid attention to her or seemed to have noticed the robed woman standing two buildings over, studying the battle. Nuala watched the woman, but the Sorcerer merely observed the fighting below. It didn't matter. She was an enemy, and Nuala had her opportunity to test her new creation.

She nudged Einar and he grunted quietly in affirmation.

With a careful eye on the target, Nuala nocked the new arrow into place and drew back her bowstring. But when she released the string, nothing happened. The arrow remained in place, hovering oddly as it held the string stretched without any pressure from her.

Because she didn't want the humans to notice, she quickly replaced her fingers so it would look like she was still aiming. Then she attempted to ease the string back and relax the arrow in its position. Nothing. The thing remained nocked and drawn, ready to fire and yet not going anywhere no matter what she tried.

A tickle of panic set in. She didn't dare turn the point away from a potential target, but she had no idea how to get the bloody thing to launch.

As she pondered her quandary, a shout rose from below. She glanced down long enough to see three of the traitor elves joining the fight, bringing a level of skill with them that the minions couldn't match—and neither could a lot of the Sinnale.

"I didn't think they fought in the battles and skirmishes, not like that," she said to Einar.

"Something must have changed. Perhaps the threat of the humans finally beating the Sorcerers. I doubt they want to be on the losing side after all this."

He sounded almost disinterested. As if the traitors meant very little to him. But she recognized all three of them. And one, many, many years ago, had been a friend. Sareena had grown resentful and mean after the wars, though. More than once she'd taken her bitterness out on Nuala, at first verbally. But twice she'd attempted to physically attack her. Those occasions had resulted in severe punishment from the king and queen, which only made Sareena's anger stronger.

When the attacks had started, Nuala had been hurt and baffled by her former friend's attitude. After the second physical attack, she'd grown angry. Well before Sareena had defected to the Sorcerers, she and Nuala had danced around each other as hostile acquaintances. When Sareena turned traitor, no one, least of all Nuala, was surprised.

Though Nuala kept the point of her arrow toward the Sorcerer, she stared down at Sareena and a deep anger rose, for her once friend, for all the traitors who'd placed their own desires above the safety of both Sinnale and Glengowyn.

"Sareena," Nuala hissed aloud, jutting her chin toward the traitor so Einar would understand her statement. Before she could say more, however, her poised arrow began to tremble. And without Nuala releasing the string, it flew from her bow.

Gasping, Nuala watched, expecting it to fly in the direction it was aimed. Instead, the arrow turned unnaturally, as if guided by an unseen hand, and flew toward the place where the traitor elves fought.

Nuala choked down a shout of dismay. There were Sinnale all around the elves. If that arrow landed among them, it would kill as many allies as enemy. And because she hadn't aimed, she had no idea who it might hit.

"Einar! What have I done?"

He stood beside her with a hand on her shoulder, watching the disaster unfold. But the arrow swerved and shivered through the chaos, actually turning to avoid hitting anyone who got in its way. The passage was impossible and defied all laws of aerodynamics. But the missile wound its way through the throngs of fighters, and to her utter astonishment, slammed directly into Sareena's chest.

The traitor looked down at the arrow, her expression almost comically surprised. Then the missile exploded in a bright flash of white light. Nuala did scream then, knowing others near Sareena would be killed too.

Instead of the mess of carnage, however, a small smoking hole dented the cobbles and the bloody remains of a single elf colored a confined area on the street. Those close to the death —minion, elf and Sinnale alike—stared without moving at the bits and pieces that were all that was left of the traitor elf. Yet no other bodies littered the ground. No one else was hurt.

The pause in fighting only lasted a beat before swords were raised again and the conflict resumed, ebbing over the dead elf and moving on. But Nuala remained frozen, too stunned to react.

After several moments, she felt the gaze of others on her. Looking up, she noticed first that the Sorcerer she'd been hoping to kill was staring at her, dark eyes wide and jaw tight. Nuala barely took note of the woman's expression before she vanished as if never having been there. The suddenness made Nuala gasp.

Einar's hand tightened on her shoulder. She turned to ask

if he'd see the Sorcerer vanish, only to realize the other archers on the rooftop were staring at her.

"We should leave," Einar said close to her ear.

She started toward the door leading from the roof. But the commander of the regiment, a short, stocky man in his middle years, approached them, blocking their exit.

"What type of arrow was that? It defied all that's logical. Can we trade for it?"

Nuala hadn't had time to figure out exactly what had happened with her new arrow, nonetheless prepared herself for a request for more. "It's…experimental and not yet ready for trade." She hoped the explanation would satisfy him.

He frowned but didn't argue. "As soon as it's ready, let us know. I'll make sure the council buys as many as we can afford."

Because she didn't know what else to say, she let Einar lead her away. The Sinnale archers turned back to their part in the battle, but she heard murmurs of curiosity and interest even as they continued the fight.

She and Einar reached the street before she spoke. "I said her name, Einar. I said Sareena's name aloud. And the arrow targeted her. I didn't have to fire it. It flew of its own accord." That realization made her clamp a hand over her mouth. "What have I done? I've just used your name aloud. What if the remaining two arrows target you?"

She wanted to throw her quiver away to keep the arrows as far from Einar as she could manage. But she was too stunned to put action to fear.

He took her shoulders in his hands and met her gaze. "Explain to me exactly how everything felt from the moment you nocked the arrow into place."

She breathed carefully and turned her senses back in time to the memories and details.

"Until I put the arrow into the bow, I didn't feel anything from it other than its bespelled nature, what I'd felt from the moment I set it," she started slowly, working past the other distractions of battle to the specific sensations. "Once I placed the arrow against the string and pulled the string back, there was a sense of…readiness. Potential. Similar to the reaction from any elf arrow."

"So until it's brought into firing position, it doesn't feel active?"

She sighed. "Maybe. When I released the string, the potential felt suspended. It was hard to tell, given the noise from the fight, but I swear I heard a low hum of…waiting. I just couldn't tell what it was waiting for."

"The name of a target."

She refocused on Einar. "When you call the owls, do you call a specific animal or just any who happen to be near?"

"Before, I could call either way—in general or specifically. Now… I'm not sure anymore. Did the arrows ever react when you said a name while in the armory?"

She frowned, her eyes narrowing. "I can't remember saying anyone's name in the armory. I must have, but… I can't be sure."

"You've said names since we followed the battle, though." He looked away for a moment. "I remember hearing you specifically say Ulric's name. I think it's safe to say that until you nock the arrow, the…seeking aspect of the spell doesn't activate."

Her shoulders drooped in relief. "So I haven't turned the remaining two into weapons aimed at you."

"I don't think so." His brow lowered. "Can you destroy these arrows? Safely. Without using them?"

"Undo the spell? I've never tried before, on any of the arrows I create. You think I should destroy these, not let them get out?"

"Not necessarily. I was just considering our options. This is an even more deadly weapon than your previous invention."

"And yet the shrapnel didn't spray out and kill those around Sareena. The destruction was focused and confined."

"An assassin's tool."

Nuala straightened. "A terrifying tool."

He took her hand. "Come. We need to return to Sinnale territory and discuss this more. But I want you away from the conflict."

She glanced back through the walls of the building, as if she could see the fighting. "Will they succeed tonight, do you think? The battle was moving in the Sinnale's favor."

"We can hope. If they drive the Sorcerers out over the next few days, there will be no need for them to request a trade in this newest weapon of yours. And I think that would be best for all."

She had to agree. The full weight of what she had created was starting to sink in, the devastation this one type of arrow could reap if placed in the wrong hands. For once, she actually agreed with her sovereigns' position on not trading her most deadly creations.

As they made their way back to the deserted streets of Noman's Land, Nuala wasn't so sure she even wanted her king and queen to know about this new weapon. If they did, she doubted they would banish her. They could hardly allow her to leave their rule given what she could now create. But would they just allow her and Einar to disobey a royal decree without punishment? Could they and still maintain the allegiance of their subjects?

A new kind of fear rolled through Nuala's gut. Suddenly banishment didn't seem so bad.

CHAPTER FIFTEEN

Once back inside Sinnale territory and safely ensconced in the council's meeting hall, Nuala and Einar made their way to the rooftop again—for both privacy and an experiment. It was time for Einar to call the owls and see how his own magics had been affected by their bond.

She settled silently at his side and waited with more patience than she thought she had left, knowing this was as important as what had happened to her magic. If he could no longer call the owls, one more aspect of his value to the king and queen vanished. Without that value, even though he remained a warrior to be feared, she couldn't be sure of the punishment they might mete out.

She almost shouted when she saw the silent, white blur in the distance, approaching steadily over the rooftops in their direction. Einar put up his arm and the owl landed gracefully. The two stared at each other for a long moment. Nuala wanted badly to speak but was afraid to distract from what was happening.

Eventually, Einar made the same soft sounds she'd heard before when speaking to the owls. There was another moment of silence. The owl screeched and Einar nodded. Then the bird launched into the air, heading back in the direction of Glengowyn.

"So," Nuala said as soon as the creature was away. "Was that a specific animal you called? Was there a difference in the communication?"

Einar leaned on the low wall circling the roof and crossed his arms over his chest, his mouth pursed in a slight frown. "The process was…different. That was a specific owl. He was actually quite far away when I called. But he came the distance, despite there being more who could have come. Apparently, the others didn't hear."

"So you can't call them generally anymore?"

"No. I can still call them generally. But now, when I'm specific, that specific animal can hear me from a much greater distance than ever before. And find me much easier without other owls passing on my position. Even a specific call before tended to be…passed between the owls. It seems that's no longer necessary."

"And the actual talking? The same or different?"

"Stronger. Clearer. I thought I could understand them perfectly before, but now… There's an added layer of meaning within our communication that was never there before. I understood him better. And he understood me better too."

"This is good!" Nuala gripped his biceps. "Stronger, better, that works in your favor. You have something the king and queen still want."

He looked down at her, his eyes dark. "You've considered that as well?"

She moved closer and he wrapped her in his arms without her having to ask. "I've considered that if they know about my newest arrows, they won't want to send me from Glengowyn. But you… We've disobeyed them. Their decree that we stay apart was no secret. Others know, and our defiance will challenge their leadership. If we bring nothing of value to earn their mercy…" She trailed off, unable to finish the sentence.

But they both knew they'd left themselves vulnerable to the same punishments placed on the traitors. If they continued to be of use to Glengowyn, however, they might just avoid the very worst possible option.

Einar tightened his hold and said aloud what she couldn't. "If they have me killed by the Sinnale, especially under the *Or'roan*, they risk killing you through the bond-link as well," he pointed out.

Though Nuala suspected Einar had been charged once or twice with assassinating another elf—secretly so that there was no evidence, only rumor—the king and queen made a point of upholding the taboo and not actually having their subjects executed by their own hands, or that of any other elf. To kill Einar would require the help of the Sinnale. But after everything the sovereigns were doing for the humans now, Nuala doubted they would object if the matter was put to them right.

"And even if you survived my death, the violent breaking of the bond could destroy this new skill of yours," he added.

"Keeping the skill or destroying it utterly would serve the same purpose—preventing others from having access to these…assassin's tools. They may not care which happens." She snuggled her head under his chin and squeezed her arms around his waist. "We should run. Now. Go as far as we can. They don't need to know about the new arrows. They can assume we took ourselves into banishment because of our bonding. They never need to know."

"And what of the arrows below in the armory? If you can't destroy them, they remain a danger." He lifted her chin with the side of his hand so she was forced to look at him. "And the humans on that rooftop witnessed the power of these arrows. Word will reach Glengowyn. We won't be safe even if we run."

She pressed her lips together to hold back the helplessness sweeping through her. "What will we do? How can we survive this?"

His large hand cupped her cheek, and he kissed her softly. But he didn't answer her questions.

NUALA SPENT THE REMAINDER OF THAT NIGHT AND MUCH OF the next day attempting to unravel the assassin spell, to destroy the arrows she'd created. The process was slow and tedious because she didn't want to kill anyone—or herself—in the process.

After some work and concentration, knowing Einar was nearby keeping watch, she managed to find the key to breaking down the spell safely. It was almost more complicated than setting the original spell had been. And it took more energy. But knowing she didn't have to leave such a deadly weapon lying about was a relief worth the energy output.

That night, after she'd managed to undo the spell on a fraction of the arrows, members of the council started to approach her. At first singly, then several of them at a time.

Rumors of the arrow she was "developing" had reached them from the front lines, where the Sinnale were slowly but steadily forcing the Sorcerers to give ground. They questioned how long it would take for the new arrows to be available, what price Glengowyn would require for them, when was the earliest date at which they could anticipate a trade arrangement?

Nuala prevaricated, never answering directly. Only saying the arrows weren't ready yet. And every time she sent the council members away, she returned to destroying more of her creations.

Einar remained a dark presence at her side, hovering and intimidating enough to keep the council from pushing her. But she knew they were working against time. News of this would reach Glengowyn soon. The council would eventually turn directly to the king and queen for real answers.

In turn, the king and queen would demand answers of their own.

When she reached the point of exhaustion, Einar made sure she slept. He saw to her needs for food and water. He kept watch when she was deep inside her magics. At the back of her mind, he was there, a safe haven in a dangerous new world.

By the second day, only about twenty of the assassin arrows remained. News reached them of the fighting and she knew the Sinnale had retaken an entire section of the city. But the forward progress had been stopped again. The Sorcerers had set new border spells the Sinnale could no longer pinpoint and avoid. And both traitor elves and Sorcerers remained beyond the reach of the shrapnel bomb arrows now, well behind the spells the humans couldn't get around to make the weapons effective.

Another standoff ensued. But the Sorcerers were on the defensive now more than ever. And a sense of satisfaction came with the stories of what was happening.

But also frustration. The council pushed a little harder for more information on her newest arrows. Would they be able to penetrate these new spells the Sorcerers had set up? How much longer before they were ready to use? Over the course of that second day, she was visited no less than five times by various humans. And each time, their interest intensified.

"I can't blame them," she told Einar during one of the breaks he forced her to take.

"Neither can I, now that they see a possible victory in sight," he said. "But I'm reluctant to have anyone know what you can do now. I'd rather you didn't even tell Ulric."

"I won't be able to lie to him if he asks directly," she admitted. "I've never been able to lie to him."

"Have you ever had cause before?"

She met his gaze. "With you. When we first mated. When we broke. I tried to keep all that to myself, but he knew. Even when I didn't say anything aloud."

Einar frowned. "Your cousin is too observant. It made him a brilliant commander during he wars, in conjunction with his talent for strategy. And I know he negotiates well with the humans in trade because of those traits. But it is inconvenient in this case."

She snorted and pointed with her dinner knife to the plate in front of him. "You eat too. You've been keeping vigil constantly since I started dismantling the arrows." She studied his face. "Have you slept at all?"

"You know I can go for long periods without sleep."

"Einar…"

Her warning actually lightened the frown creasing his brows and crinkling his eyes. An almost-smile lifted the corners of his mouth. "I find it…unusual, how you worry about me. I'm not used to it. At least not from anyone but you."

"You know well why I worry."

"And I love you too."

She rolled her eyes and smiled. "That, unfortunately, is part of our problem."

"But the best part," he said, gripping her hand in a tight squeeze. He released her and gestured back to her plate, a not-so-subtle reminder for her to continue her meal. "I have been considering the Sinnale's interest in your weapon, the weapon itself… Has it occurred to you that if they had the names of the individual Sorcerers, it might be possible to kill them without having to engage in all-out offensives anymore?"

"Yes, actually. In the midst of all their questions, I did consider that. But they'd need the Sorcerers' real names. Not what they go by, not what the minions call them. Their true names."

"You're sure?"

"I learned a lot more about the spell during the dismantling. Knowing what the trigger is has given me an insight that's let me understand the workings of the magic better. The arrow that killed Sareena wouldn't have flown without her real name."

"So much has happened…" He paused, studying her for a

quiet moment. "Are you sorry about that killing? Once again you've been forced to break the taboo. Are there regrets?"

She tilted her head. She'd been so concerned with the dangerous weapon she'd made she'd barely considered that she'd taken yet another elf's life. That others had witnessed her doing what elves were not supposed to be able to do.

"I hadn't thought about that until now," she admitted. "Not only have I created an assassin's weapon, but the humans saw me kill another elf. They know about the taboo. They think it's impossible for us to kill one another. Now that they've seen that's not the case... I'm not sure what this means."

"I'm more concerned with how you're feeling about it. The humans and what they believe or don't believe holds no real interest for me."

"I don't regret Sareena's death," she said, and knew she told only the truth. "The traitors forfeit their right to my sympathy. And the longer I'm in Sinnale, the more firmly I feel about that. These people have been our allies for centuries, since settling near Glengowyn. I will never understand or forgive the traitors' defection."

"I'm glad to hear it. I would not see you suffer for killing one who would, given the chance, hand you over to the Sorcerers."

"All the killing... Have you ever felt remorse?" she asked.

"No." His tone was flat and matter-of-fact. "I'm not sure I have it in me. It seems to be part of the same aspect of me that becomes...what I become in the heat of battle. Sometimes..." He trailed off and looked away.

She reached across to take hold of his hand this time, snapping his attention back to her. "Sometimes?"

"I suspect it's a…fault in my character that I can't feel regret for the deaths I bring. I should have some emotional reaction to it. Don't you think?"

"Why? You've only ever killed those threatening your people, right? You've never killed for pleasure or fun. You don't kill simply to kill. Where is there any call for regrets?"

He tilted his head as if he'd never considered her points and blinked slowly. "Other warriors, after the wars, talked about the…effect all the death had on them. I never experienced those same scars."

"I actually envy you that."

"So you do regret killing the two traitors?"

"No, no. Not them. But at the start of the war, when my mistake in transporting the shrapnel arrows cost so many elves their lives? I've always felt a great deal of guilt about that. They were senseless, pointless deaths. But the traitors… No. With Sareena, I only felt a rage for her betrayal. When the arrow flew, I was terrified I'd kill the Sinnale surrounding her. *That* I would have regretted. But I just don't seem to feel anything at all for her death."

Einar's frown turned fierce. "I have passed that to you too with our bonding," he growled and stood to pace away from her. "The king was right to order me away from you. I have… infected you with my greatest fault."

"Einar, don't be ridiculous. Even before the bond took hold, I had no regrets about killing Byral. You haven't 'infected' me with anything. Perhaps this is *my* character flaw. I'm not a warrior. Shouldn't I be more affected by killing? Yet I'm not. I say that speaks very poorly of my conscience."

She blinked and he'd crossed the room to loom over her.

"Never say such things. You are the most honorable and

beautiful soul I've ever known." He leaned down, putting his face close to hers. "And I will not have you speaking poorly of yourself."

He was so fierce in his defense of her, she warmed all the way to her core. Taking his face in her hands, she touched her nose to his and said, "I feel the same of you. So stop talking of 'infecting' me, or I will have to get very cross with you."

She kissed him to silence any protest he might make. As she swept her tongue into his mouth to tangle with his, she grew more and more annoyed that he would dare to insult his own character as he had. And then feel he could reprimand her for the same comments!

She took her annoyance out on him, standing to press tight to him and kissing him with a fierce possessiveness she'd never felt for any other man.

His arms tightened around her waist as she felt the *Shaerta* rising. And a thrill of satisfaction roared into her blood.

"You are good," she said between kisses. "And you will never think otherwise while I live."

She trailed hot, openmouthed kisses down his throat, nipping and biting, tasting the salt on his skin. "I love you, Einar. For everything you are."

"And I you." He tightened his hold in a convulsive hug before moving his hands to her ass and grinding her tight against his erection.

The feel of him, hard and solid, was a balm to her fears, regrets and lack of regrets. Though they were still in the armory, though the door was only nominally sealed since they were eating, she wanted him. There and then. To feel the rightness between them, letting the significance of what they had override all the other doubts and complications.

He didn't resist as she backed him up to the wall, only grunted when they hit the solid stone a little harder than she'd intended. But he never loosened his hold on her or stopped kissing her.

He ravaged her mouth, giving her exactly what she needed, what she wanted from him. Hard hands, desperate demands. Her tunic came up over her head with barely a break in their contact. She ripped material as she stripped off his shirt and vest. The heat of his skin enveloped her, making her moan as she rubbed her breasts against him.

She would have easily, happily fucked him against the wall, but he shifted and angled her toward the small cot she'd been using to nap on between magical sessions. Before laying her down, he dropped to his knees and wrenched off her trousers and boots. He licked into her core while still removing her clothing, and the feel of his tongue circling her clit sent a tremor of shockwaves through her body, making her knees quake.

After he stripped her completely, he moved from her sensitive clit back up her body along her stomach, kissing and licking skin now sensitive enough to ache with the pleasure. His teeth closed around her nipple, and he tugged gently before he licked away the brief sting. Then he sucked her nipple into his mouth, the heat and pull causing a fresh wave of wetness between her legs. She moaned, burying her hands in his hair as her hips jerked in reaction.

By the time he reached her mouth, she could taste her own skin, her own juices on his lips, and the flavor mixing with his moved her beyond needy to desperate. Though she attempted to assist him with his trousers, he pushed her hands aside and stripped quickly and efficiently himself. And then they were on the bed with his weight anchoring her to the mattress.

She couldn't have him inside her fast enough, couldn't taste or feel or squeeze enough, as the *Shaerta* drove them harder and harder. He slammed into her in a single thrust, and she arched up under him, stifling a shout. He filled her completely, in every possible way, and she welcomed every beloved inch.

He wasn't gentle. She refused to be tender. She wanted him out of control, wanted to lose control herself. And only with Einar was she safe enough to completely let go.

She bit his shoulder to keep from crying out when her first orgasm hit. He reacted to the feel of her teeth by pounding harder into her, his own groan muffled against her throat. The increased speed and the feel of his coarse hair rubbing her clit sent her into a second orgasm almost immediately, only ever possible with Einar, even under the full influence of the *Shaerta*. She couldn't hold back her shout this time and no longer cared if the entire hall heard them.

Digging her nails into his back, anchoring her heels on the backs of his legs, she clenched and thrust and chased his rhythm, feeling him storming to his own breaking point. And when he hit that edge and threw himself off, she ground against him and came again, her body so awash in sensation all she knew for long moments was the spasms and euphoria of release in Einar's arms.

They ended their dance more slowly than they'd started, panting and clinging to one another, warm in the heat they'd generated. She hugged him tight, refusing to let go, keeping him inside her for as long as possible.

Her brain would have happily shut down, but behind the contentment and sleepiness, the nagging thought remained to follow her into a doze—they couldn't delay facing the king and queen for much longer.

Shortly after they woke up, they received word from Glengowyn via a messenger owl.

Their presence was required at Court.

CHAPTER SIXTEEN

$\mathcal{N}$uala stood with her back straight, careful not to touch Einar as they faced their king and queen side by side. They'd been given time to change and ready themselves, but not much longer before the Court guards came to collect them for their audience.

Silence hung heavily over the area. Surrounded by trees dripping with foliage, the Court was open to the air but sheltered from inclement weather by the thickness of the trees and one of the king's spells. The thrones themselves weren't all that grand—simple affairs of wood and soft cushions, set with winking jewels peeking from between the twists and turns of the wood. Neither the king nor queen required a background of grandeur to reflect their power. The very simplicity of the Court highlighted just how spectacular the royal couple was.

Nuala had never been so nervous in her life. She wanted desperately to grasp Einar's hand, for support and comfort. But she didn't dare. She held herself motionless and waited for her sovereigns to begin—she was forbidden by Court etiquette from speaking first but wouldn't have even if she could.

She found it impossible to read either of their facial expressions. Though that wasn't unusual, it was the first time those blank, neutral masks had been directed at her while she knew she was facing punishment.

The queen was stunning, her hair a silken cloak around her shoulders, several shades darker than the lightest blonds in Glengowyn but full of sparkling life like it was a creature all its own. Her face was narrow, her cheekbones sharp, her full lips set in a neutral line, her eyes a piercing violet that was unusual among the Glengowyn elves. She had her long-fingered hands resting at the edge of the armrests on her throne, and the single ring she wore—a bejeweled indication of her position—winked in the glowing bluish-white lights coming from the surrounding trees.

The king was almost innocuous in his appearance, if one didn't take the time to really look at him. He was of average height for an elf, with hip-length brown hair and dark eyes that tilted up just a little at the corners. His jaw was solid and his lips thin and firm. The golden torc around his throat, which announced his position, highlighted the firm musculature of his upper body, at once powerful and understated beneath his heavy silk tunic.

His power emanated from him in an unseen aura, breathtaking in its strength. Simply standing before him had driven many an elf humbly to their knees without the king having to raise a finger or exert any magical force.

Together, the royal couple had ruled Glengowyn since

well before Nuala's parents had been born. They had a timeless feel about them that brooked no disobedience.

And here she stood, having disobeyed them because she could no longer deny her love for Einar.

Just as their silence stretched her nerves to the snapping point, the queen spoke.

"We are disappointed, Nuala. Einar. Our position on your relationship was clear."

Nuala ducked her head in a slight bow without taking her eyes off the queen's face. To look away was to open herself up to an unexpected attack.

"Your Majesty," she said, as firmly and humbly as she could manage, "my magic still produces the weapons you wished to protect. Despite our...lapse, you have not lost anything that I can give to Glengowyn."

"We understand that contrary to losing, you have gained," the king said, the deep power of his voice commanding her attention. "The council is asking if we will trade in this 'experimental' weapon of yours."

She swallowed and risked a glance around the hall. Other elves circled the perimeter, members of the Court, important advisors to the sovereigns. This hearing wasn't open to all of Glengowyn, but she wasn't sure how much to say out loud, how much the royal couple would want her to admit in front of the audience.

"My magics have been...affected by the bonding, Your Majesty. A new type of arrow has been created."

"And this arrow does what, exactly?" the queen asked.

Nuala still couldn't read either of their moods from their expressions. The lack of feedback tightened the tension crawling through her gut. She made a point of gesturing to the surrounding Court and asked, "May I explain now? Or would you prefer a private explanation?"

"That deadly?" the king murmured.

"That dangerous," she affirmed as quietly as she could.

For the first time, a slight expression broke through the king's neutrality. His features didn't exactly change, but she thought she detected a hint of approval in his eyes.

"Should we share such a weapon with the Sinnale, do you think?" the queen asked, her demeanor still scarily neutral.

"I would leave that decision to the wisdom of Your Majesties."

"Of course it will be our decision. Would these weapons compromise Glengowyn if we were to share them with the humans?"

Nuala was silent for a long moment. Without explaining what the arrows could do, she wasn't sure how to answer. "These weapons are deadly in any hands. Elf and human alike."

Queen Rohannah tilted her head to one side. "You imply elves could use them…in unforeseen ways?"

"I state outright that these are the most *specifically* dangerous arrows I have ever created."

The queen's eyes narrowed, having caught the emphasis Nuala placed on the word "specifically".

She exchanged a look with her king, then swept her gaze over the Court. Immediately, the area cleared so that only the guards remained. Then she turned her piercing violet gaze on Nuala.

"Explain 'specifically'."

Nuala did, revealing not only what the arrow had done, but that she'd killed another elf with it. She didn't mention that she'd managed to kill a traitor elf when they'd first been attacked, and she didn't bring up the fact that she'd witnessed Einar kill an elf.

It was enough for their small remaining audience to know that a humble weapons maker had been able to kill another elf simply by murmuring that elf's name to an arrow.

"So. An assassin's instrument, then," the king said.

"Just so, Your Majesty," she affirmed.

"Would this arrow destroy a Sorcerer?" the queen asked.

Nuala tilted her head to one side, not surprised the queen had hit on the same possibility she and Einar had discussed earlier.

"We would require their *real* names for that to work," she said. "But I do think it's possible. Gaining a Sorcerer's real name is problematic." More like impossible, but she didn't think it wise to say so in that moment. "But the real name of any being would be enough, based on my analysis of the spell."

"How many of these weapons did you create?" The queen again.

She swallowed, not sure if this news would be greeted with approval or disappointment. "I created, in total, just short of three hundred individual arrows, and I have destroyed all but five."

"Destroyed?" The king's eyebrow lifted slightly, his only visible reaction.

"I dismantled the spell and took the arrows themselves apart."

"Because?"

"I felt them too dangerous to leave with the Sinnale when they weren't aware of their potential."

The king drummed his fingers once on his armrest, and again Nuala thought she saw a hint of something like approval in his eyes.

He and the queen exchanged another long look, silent but intent. Nuala tried to stay calm, but her heartbeat hammered and her skin tingled from the nervous energy consuming her. When the royal couple faced them again, she had to force herself not to hold her breath.

"This news, this accomplishment of yours, will affect what we do with you going forward, Nuala," the queen announced. "Your disobedience, and the disobedience of our own Darkness, cannot go unpunished."

Nuala dipped her knee in a slight bow of acknowledgement.

"Darkness—" the queen turned just her gaze on Einar, "—how has the bonding affected your skills? The owls?"

"Still respond to me, Your Majesty. The way in which we communicate has…heightened, but that ability has not been destroyed."

"And yet, I am not sure it's enough to satisfy," she said. "You were our most trusted guard. And you have publicly gone against our orders. This cannot be allowed to stand. Even though we will lose one of our most dangerous allies."

Einar remained unmoving, taking her words in without comment or gesture, patient as always when standing before his king and queen.

"You two have left us in an untenable position." The queen spoke quietly. "Banishment is no longer an option. Nuala's newest ability is too dangerous to go unmonitored. But punishment is necessary."

Her gaze lifted by the barest of flickers, and a moment

later, Nuala and Einar were dragged apart by the rough hands of several guards.

Instinctively, Nuala resisted. "Einar…"

He allowed himself to be pulled away from her, but he kept his attention on her now, rather than the royal couple.

"Darkness," the queen intoned. "Your willful disobedience to this Court requires a severe penalty. But which is best? Banishment, the *Or'roan*… Simple banishment would be unwise, given that Nuala will remain here in Glengowyn under our supervision. I do not think you would stay away."

He didn't say anything.

"The *Or'roan* and banishment together would, likewise, hardly concern you now that you have bonded with Nuala."

While he didn't confirm this statement, Nuala saw in his eyes that the queen spoke truthfully.

"You leave us with one option, Darkness. Banishment to the Unseen Plain—"

"No!" Nuala cried out, unable to stop her protest.

That was worse than even a simple death sentence. A punishment that had never been used in Nuala's lifetime. In fact, she couldn't recall any time in her parents' or grandparents' lifetimes when the punishment had been invoked. Nuala hadn't even considered that her sovereigns might use it now.

It meant more than having Einar killed by a human assassin—to preserve the illusion that elves didn't kill each other. Einar would suffer a horrendous, painful death as the *dargem*, those nightmare-inducing creatures that called the Unseen Plain their home, slowly ate and digested him. They weren't just talking about taking his life. They spoke of inflicting one of the worst tortures possible on him before he died.

The queen ignored her outburst. "And you will be sent under the *Or'roan*. Your disobedience cannot be forgiven. The punishment must be severe."

"Please, Your Majesty, not that," Nuala begged, facing her queen. "Killing Einar now could affect my magic more even than the bonding. Would you lose your most dangerous weapon?"

She settled her violet-eyed gaze on Nuala without even blinking. "We will be losing one of our most dangerous weapons already, Nuala. Because of your selfishness and inability to do what we have ordered."

"Please, Your Majesty, not the Unseen Plain."

"Would you take his place?" she asked very quietly.

"Yes," Nuala said without hesitation. "I would take his place. Even under the *Or'roan*, I would suffer the Unseen Plain if Einar could live."

"No," Einar said, his voice deep and resonant, echoing in its quiet intensity.

The queen raised her brows, the first indication of any sort of emotion. "You have presented us with an interesting option, Nuala. This arrow you've created might be too dangerous to allow into the world. If you are no longer on this plane, you can no longer create such a threat."

She swallowed but straightened her shoulders. The move did nothing to loosen the grip of the guards holding her arms. "Yes, Your Majesty. You could eliminate a possible threat, make the severity of disobeying your orders an example to the rest of Glengowyn, and retain your Darkness. Simply by allowing me to die in Einar's place."

"No," Einar said again, his voice rising only slightly above a reverberating growl.

The queen continued to ignore him. "You make a very good point. Though we would hate to lose your value to us, Nuala, even you are not above our judgment. This would be a good lesson for the others."

"Yes, Your Majesty."

The queen turned on Einar, considering. "This would be a severe punishment for you too, I believe, Darkness. One that would also resonate with the others. We will strip you of that which you value most as punishment for your treachery." She blinked slowly. "Yes. That is much more severe than even death for you, my warrior. An important lesson for the rest of Glengowyn. No matter your station, there will be consequences for disobeying our rule."

Nuala watched Einar's muscles flex against the hold of the two guards, and in an instant, four more surrounded him, their swords drawn and pointed at various vulnerable parts of his body, even as the first two continued to hold him in place. His expression shifted, and she saw the first stirrings of the madness that took him in battle coming over him.

"Einar," she murmured.

He held her gaze, his entire body tensed, as they awaited the final proclamation.

CHAPTER SEVENTEEN

Nuala once again found herself holding her breath, but she couldn't look away from Einar, even when King Varim spoke.

"Do you offer an alternative, Darkness?" the king asked.

"My life, Your Majesty. My existence. Anything you would take from me. Only that you do not send Nuala to the kind of death she would meet on the Unseen Plain."

Another long silence stretched Nuala's nerves. She jerked against the two guards confining her because she had to do something physical or she might just scream.

Finally, the queen said, "For the sovereignty of this Court and the safety of Glengowyn, there is only one answer. Nuala of Glengowyn, you will be banished to the Unseen Plain at dawn, under the *Or'roan*. Einar, you will be witness to this punishment. Your life, your existence, doomed to continue long after you watch Nuala sent to her end."

Nuala began to tremble and a single tear escaped the corner of her eye. Her knees weakened at the thought of what she was going to face, but she tightened the muscles in her thighs to keep upright. Einar couldn't be allowed to see her fear. She would accept the punishment as stoically as she could manage, because it meant Einar would live.

More than any other regret, though, she regretted that she would never know Einar again. That they had had so very little time together.

"I love you," she mouthed as the guards began to haul her away.

They'd barely moved two steps when the battle madness swept over Einar's face.

"No!" His voice roared through the hall, shaking the leaves on the trees, making even Nuala jump in surprise.

He folded his body in tight, bringing the guards close. Swords began to poke into him, positioned to hurt and draw blood rather than kill. But before more than one could penetrate his skin, he cried out another denial and threw his arms wide. The elves surrounding him went flying in all directions, slamming hard into trees, smashing into limp heaps on the smooth stone covering the ground.

He turned to the guards holding her, his eyes blacker than she'd ever seen, and he shouted another denial. The two elves holding her catapulted backward, ripped from her side by invisible hands to be flattened to the ground at the edge of the clearing, their bodies unmoving.

Nuala barely had time to register what had happened before Einar closed the space between them and swung her behind his back as he faced the royal couple.

"You will not send Nuala to the Unseen Plain," he ground out, his voice so deep it was almost unrecognizable.

He barely sounded like a man anymore, something so

vicious and deadly crawled through his tone. The sound raised the hairs on Nuala's arms and made her shiver despite herself. She couldn't see his face well, but the all-consuming rage in his expression before he stepped in front of her had been one of the most awesome and terrifying things she'd ever witnessed. And she'd seen Einar at his battle-crazed worst. Without a weapon in hand, the man before her seemed more deadly even than the *dargem* she would face when banished.

The king raised his brows, his only outward reaction to the sudden and explosive chaos. But the queen… Nuala would have sworn she was seeing things. The queen smiled. A very slight lifting of the corners of her mouth, true, but it was, nonetheless, a smile. Her eyes narrowed and sparked. And Nuala got the distinct and disconcerting feeling the queen was…pleased.

"I wondered what it would take, Darkness. You are so difficult to push to this state. I should have guessed earlier the answer would be so simple. You've only ever had but one weakness."

"I don't understand." Nuala dug her fingers into Einar's arm, fear for what he'd done, what he'd become, a tight band around her chest.

"What I am in battle," he said, his voice sounding more normal, his attention still on the queen, "apparently it is part of my magic."

"So much a part of him, even he couldn't tell," the queen affirmed. "And now… Now, my Darkness, you are a killing machine."

"What does she mean?" Nuala asked, looking up at the side of his face. His jaw was stiff, his expression unmoving.

"I could have killed the guards," he explained. "I did not.

But I could have. Without using a weapon other than my own rage."

She looked at the fallen guards then back up at him. "You can…explode your rage now, like my shrapnel arrows? Because of the bonding?"

He jerked his head in a single nod.

"But…"

"The melding of your magics," the queen said. "His ability to communicate with the owls is not the only thing that was strengthened." She stared at Einar, again with that pleased, small smile. "He can now level armies without having to remove his sword from its scabbard."

"Very useful," the king said, finally commenting aloud. "Very useful, I should think."

The queen leaned back in her throne, looking for all the world as if she was quite satisfied with this outcome.

"I still don't understand," Nuala said. "What does this mean?"

Even as she asked, the Court began to fill. Not with elves but with owls. They perched on the surrounding trees, flittering but silent witnesses. As Nuala looked around at the descending birds, she realized that, outside of the king, queen, herself, Einar and the unconscious bodies of the guards Einar had attacked, there were no other elves in the Court. The remaining guards had vanished.

She looked back to the queen, who was fully smirking now as she considered the owls.

"Silly girl," she said to Nuala. "Do you think we would have placed you and Einar in such close proximity, after all this time, if we did not have a plan?"

Einar straightened and some of the defensiveness went out of his body. "You intended for us to bond. Why?"

"Beyond growing tired of watching you two mope around this city for the last two centuries?" She snorted, an unusual show of irritated humor. "Let's just say that the possibilities of your bonding were revealed to me. And the time for the change was now."

The queen had mysterious ways of gathering information, sometimes even gaining knowledge of things that had not yet happened. She didn't exercise the skill often, or so Nuala had thought. And the way in which she gathered the information was a mystery. Nuala wasn't even sure if the king knew what the queen did to gain this future sight. But it wasn't a flawless skill.

"You took a great risk," she said as Einar finally allowed her to step out from behind the protection of his body.

"Yes, she did," the king growled. "But the gamble has been well worth the risk, I think."

"Just so, my love," the queen said. "Just so."

"You knew I would create a new arrow?"

"That part was more...nebulous. We knew something powerful would come through you in the bonding."

And suddenly Nuala understood. "But you knew the bonding would affect Einar's fighting ability. That it was part of his magic, even though he didn't realize it. And the blending of our two magics would strengthen his deadliness. You knew what he would become."

The queen could read magic in others, detect spells and see through to the core of an elf. These were traits well known throughout Glengowyn and skills she utilized often. Nuala should have guessed her ability to see the magic inside them all would also affect the knowledge she gained through her future sight.

"And because of my gamble," the queen said, "you have been allowed your love. But there are conditions." Suddenly her satisfied expression fell away and was replaced by the terrifying seriousness she'd worn earlier.

"You have both become more valuable to us," the queen continued. "And at the same time have brought with you skills that are so dangerous, they cannot be allowed free reign."

"You will pledge your loyalty and these new skills to us and Glengowyn," the king said. "For our use alone. On pain of forever death by public and painful means if you should disobey."

"We will make it plain to the city that your bonding was intended. That we saw the magics that would be created." The queen took up the telling. "And you will not contradict us. You will, in fact, say that you were given permission to renew your relationship. No one will disagree with you."

Nuala looked up as the owls fluttered their wings in the treetops. She'd almost forgotten them in her shock.

"We will direct the use of your new skills," the king said, yanking Nuala's attention back down to him. "And you will obey us in our orders going forward."

"In exchange," the queen said, "you have your lives, your bonding and your futures. A fair exchange, I think."

This last she murmured, and Nuala heard the warning just beneath the simple statement.

"Your Majesties," she said, dropping to one knee and bowing her head. "I will give you everything you ask and pledge my loyalty forward, in exchange for the prize of being able to keep Einar."

For a long moment, Einar remained standing, staring at his king and queen. Finally, he too knelt down, though he didn't bow his head. "For the love of Nuala, I will continue to serve you faithfully as my sovereigns. From now until I move to the next plane."

The king nodded in satisfaction. The queen merely blinked her approval.

"Now," the king said after the formalities had been seen to. "Nuala. I would like to discuss this new arrow of yours. And how it might best be used to rid our region of the Sorcerers."

THE SUN THREW SPECKS OF PINK AND ORANGE LIGHT ACROSS the forest floor as Einar escorted Nuala back to her small home at the very center of the city. He kept his arm around her, holding her close as they strolled down the quiet stone paths leading to her front door.

"I'm not entirely sure how I feel now," she said, her voice low in deference to the quiet time of day. The beauty of it, the fact that they were alive and together was almost more than her heart could take. But how they'd gotten here…

"If you feel the same annoyance and anger I do, I would not blame you," Einar said.

"And yet, it's all come out for the best."

"After much torment and two centuries of waste."

She couldn't blame him for the low growl in his voice. She was torn between her own gratitude and anger. "Will you be able to serve them with the same loyalty as before?"

"My loyalty is to you now, and only you. That hasn't

changed. But for you, I will serve them to the best of my ability, with all my strength and honor. They know this."

A tiny thrill of pleasure warred with an even tinier worry that his changed allegiance might not sit well with the sovereigns. But if they knew…

She let the worry go for now. She was too tired to contemplate disasters that weren't currently a problem. Instead, she asked two of the many questions she had about the previous night. "If the queen knew what would become of our bonding, why did she make us wait so long? Why make us suffer for so many years?"

With his free hand, Einar lifted one of her hands and placed a kiss on her palm. The feel of his mouth on her skin sent tingles up her arm.

"I asked the queen those very questions when you and the king were discussing the details of your new arrows."

"What did she say?"

"I quote: 'Your bonding was required at this point in time, my Darkness.'"

Nuala waited a few steps but when he didn't continue, she said, "That's all? Our bonding was required now? Does that mean she knew all along? That she only gained the knowledge of how our bonding would change our magic recently? Was this all hope and presumption on her part? Have they allowed us to remain brokenhearted all this time at a whim or because the movements of the universe required it? I don't understand."

"She said no more on the subject and refused to explain further. I have no clue if she knew all along or if she only realized recently what our bonding would mean. And that it was as important to them as it was to us."

They stopped just outside her front door, and Einar turned her to face him. "I do know that I'm unhappy about being kept from you for so long. But grateful to have you now. Freely. Without any threats hanging over our heads."

"Unless we break our new vow of fealty to the sovereigns," she pointed out.

"Do you intend to? Would you want to?"

Her first response was sharp and sarcastic, but she held that reaction back while she really thought about her feelings on the matter.

"No," she said after a few moments. "No. I'm still loyal to them, despite what's happened. I do want my skills to benefit Glengowyn always. Though I could do without the label of being 'too valuable', I recognize my value to the city and would continue to serve."

"And so long as you serve them, I will without restraint. You were my only point of contention with the sovereigns, ever. I will continue to protect them with all I have." He cupped her cheeks. "But they come second to you. I made that clear to them before we left this morning."

She gripped his wrists as a tingle of fear tickled her nap. Perhaps this disaster was more imminent than she'd thought. "How did they react?" The queen was notorious for taking the elevation of others above her…poorly.

"The king said nothing, only raised his brows."

"As he does," she commented with a sideways dip of her head.

"The queen smiled."

"Smiled?"

"And then said, and again I will quote, 'Why do you

believe this is information new to us, Darkness? What has changed to make this different?'"

Nuala gasped. And then she laughed. "She's always known? That you would choose me over them?"

He kissed her lightly. "Apparently, you are my only vulnerability. And she used that knowledge willfully."

Nuala rose up to kiss him this time, letting her mouth slide across his in comfort and love. "I won't take advantage of being your only vulnerability," she promised with her lips close enough to brush his as she spoke. "Just remember, you're mine as well. Take care with my heart."

"Your heart will never be safer than with me," he vowed. "Through all our lifetimes. You're mine, Nuala. My only love. And I'll hold our bonding sacred into the end times."

She sighed and relaxed fully against him, absorbing his kiss like oxygen, like the very essence of her existence. A part of her still couldn't believe they were free, to love, to be together, to live. But the larger part of her rejoiced. Two centuries of pain and loss dribbled away as she led Einar into her home, into her bed, and gave over fully to the perfect sense of their love.

As morning sun spilled across her bed and Einar slid gently inside her, Nuala embraced the man others called Darkness, knowing, to her, he would always be her light.

**Continue reading for an excerpt from
the next book in
the Fire and Tears series**

DAWN IGNITED

Fire & Tears
Book Three

DAWN IGNITED

Author Kat Simons writing as

ISABO KELLY

DAWN IGNITED

FIRE AND TEARS BOOK THREE

EXCERPT

CHAPTER 1

lthir of Glengowyn stared at Samuel Brightarrow for a long moment after hearing his proposition. The man had aged over the last two years, the ongoing war with the Sorcerers taking its toll on the once large and vibrant human. Samuel and his wife Iona, members of the Sinnale council, were the reason Althir found himself here, a prisoner of the Sinnale.

The reason he wasn't forever dead.

"This might be your only chance at redemption, Althir," Samuel said in his deep, even voice.

Althir snorted. "Redemption." He shouldn't need redemption now. He should have had everything he ever wanted, and instead he spent his days wasting away in this comfortably maddening cage in the basement of the Sinnale council's meeting hall.

"Ulric has spoken with the king and queen. They've agreed to allow you back to Glengowyn if you complete this task."

"And why would I want to go back?" Althir paced away from the man. "Labeled a traitor by my fellow elves for all time? There's nothing there for me."

"Then you'd be free to go wherever you please. Another elven city, perhaps. But you wouldn't be a prisoner any longer."

He didn't bother to answer. His bespelled cage wasn't the worst thing that could have happened to him. And what would he do with freedom? No other elven community would welcome him once they learned of his history.

He glanced out the high window at the sliver of blue sky above the hard lines of brick making up the neighboring building that blocked most of his view. Ah, but he did miss the forest. He'd had enough of this bloody besieged city, the place where his entire life had been ruined.

"Speaking of Ulric," he said to change the subject, and because he couldn't quite help himself. "How is my brother, anyway? Never does come to visit. I imagine he's too busy fucking your daughter. Though, I can hardly blame him. She is infinitely fuckable." He stared at Samuel as he said this last, watching his reaction.

Samuel stared back. His pale skin darkened and his eyes narrowed. Althir smirked.

Rather than the explosion of anger he'd been expecting, though, Samuel calmly said, "You're trying to send me away in a fury. You want me to refuse you this chance. Why?"

Althir curled his lip in a snarl. He'd never hated another being more in his entire life than he hated Samuel in that moment. For being too wise and seeing too much.

He stalked as far away from the man as he could get, keeping his focus on the sliver of blue sky.

"You're mad to trust me with this," he stated flatly, his back to Samuel. "Why would you do that?"

"You know their Citadel. You know where to find what we need."

True. He did. They only knew the List of Names was there —that it existed at all— because of him.

But the mission was suicide. Since he was no longer under the *Or'roan*, the forever death curse that robbed elves of all future lives, ending their existence permanently, death didn't frighten him. He was just infuriated that he found himself in this bloody position.

Suicide or a cage for the foreseeable future? What kinds of choices were those? Although, if he succeeded, he'd be responsible for ending this war once and for all. Would that change anything?

Would that give him back what he'd lost?

"You'll trust me to return if I do succeed?" He was actually quite curious about the answer. He'd been providing the Sinnale with good information for months now, information that had helped turned the war in their favor and put the Sorcerers on the defensive. But the fighting dragged on. Humans continued to die. They wanted the fighting done, he knew. Would that desire override their continued wariness of him?

"You should know better than that, Althir," Samuel said. "Someone will be going with you. Someone who will ensure you return."

"An elf?"

"A Sinnale volunteer."

He laughed, a sharp, bitter sound. "A volunteer? Suicidal, are they?"

Samuel was silent, and Althir didn't push the subject. The "volunteer" hardly mattered anyway. He didn't care who they were or why they'd go on this impossible quest into the section of the city under the Sorcerers' control.

When the silence had stretched for long moments and Althir still didn't turn to face Samuel, Samuel finally said, "You have until tomorrow to consider our offer. I'll return at midday for your answer."

"There's no need," he said, his voice harsh and echoing in the quiet room.

"You're refusing? You won't accept this chance?"

"Oh, I'll go. Suicide or not. I don't really have a choice, do I?"

Very quietly, Samuel said, "You've always had a choice, Althir. It was those choices that got you here."

Althir didn't acknowledge the comment with so much as a twitch of his shoulders. He continued to stare out the window until well after he'd heard the cage door open and close behind Samuel. He stared out his little window until the light faded and the blue sky turned a purple bruised smudge against the hard, sharp city bricks.

MINA WATCHED THE ELF FOR A LONG TIME FROM HER POSITION at the opposite side of the huge basement. His cage, a literal cage of bars mixed with minerals and magic to keep an elf contained, was furnished with a comfortable bed, a desk, a small bookshelf fully stocked with what the Sinnale had to offer, a washbasin and stand, and another table where he could eat. The trunk at the foot of his bed was full of clean clothes.

And the nearest stone walls were hung with thick, colorful tapestries to keep out some of the cold.

She resented all that luxury for a prisoner, a traitor. Yes, he was giving them information to help in the war now. But that didn't forgive the fact that he'd turned traitor to Glengowyn and Sinnale by joining forces with the Sorcerers all those many months ago. She knew the only reason he'd turned himself over to her people was to save his sorry hide from the Sinnale assassins.

She had no sympathy for him, despite how beautiful he looked in the pale gaslight leaking in through the high window that had been his sole focus for most of the afternoon.

In fact, his beauty only made her angrier. How could someone so cruel, so wicked, look so stunning and enticing? It shouldn't have been possible. She shouldn't notice the solid strength of his shoulders, or the firm lines of a body that filled his trousers so nicely. She should be able to see beyond the masculine planes of his face and the stunning contrast of his angled gray eyes against his long, dark hair.

His brother was allowed to be gorgeous. Ulric was actively working with the Sinnale and the human council to help them win the war and rid their city of the invading Sorcerers. She admired Ulric, and a small part of her envied Layla Brightarrow her mate. But Althir was nothing like his brother.

Her fascination with the elf wasn't purely for his looks, though, and she consoled herself with that. She was preoccupied with him for other reasons, reasons that had more to do with revenge and anger than desire. Emotions she would now have to control if she wanted to see their mission successfully completed.

An end to this horrible war, which had robbed her of so much, was worth putting her personal hatred aside. She wouldn't attempt to kill Althir. She would go with him into enemy territory, as she'd sworn to do, and ensure he returned to her people with the List of Names. Once that was done, however, the elf could rot in the worst torments of the sacred hells for all she cared.

He finally turned away from the window, and she caught sight of his profile in the weak light. Her breath hitched. Reminding her once again that the face of a god could hide the soul of a demon.

"You might as well come out of the shadows," he said, staring at her hiding spot.

She knew he couldn't see her. Still, he seemed to look directly into her eyes as he spoke.

"Who are you and why are you here?" he asked, seeming only half interested in the response.

She straightened her shoulders and approached the cage, coming into the weak light filtering through the windows. Before answering, she took the time to turn up some of the small lamps that provided light in the basement. Having this conversation in the dark felt too intimate, and she was in no mood to be vulnerable for the traitor.

When she was comfortable with the bright lighting, she faced Althir. "I'm Mina," she said, answering his first question because it was the easiest.

"What's your family name, Mina?" His mouth remained a flat line, his eyes revealing very little real interest in her.

"I no longer have any family to be named. Thanks to the war." *Thanks to you and the Sorcerers.*

He nodded and sprawled in the chair next to his desk. "Of course you don't. I wouldn't let it bother you much. Family is highly overrated."

She curled her lip, unable to keep the reaction to herself. In her mind, she cursed him into the next world and beyond. Outwardly, she remained silent, not wishing to give him any more reaction than she already had.

He stared at her for a long moment, the disinterest in his gaze sharpening to something more alert. "So what do you want, Mina of No Family?"

"Your death."

She waited for him to react. He didn't. She realized this probably wasn't the first time one of her people had said that to him.

With a shrug, she seated herself on a "visitors" chair outside his cell. "What I intend to do, however, is just the opposite."

That finally earned her a raised brow. "Am I to assume you're the 'volunteer' accompanying me into Sorcerer territory?"

She dipped her head in a single brief nod.

"And what makes you think you'll fare any better than the rest of your family?"

"Nothing."

"You're prepared to die?"

For the first time, he seemed genuinely interested in her response. His head tilted to one side as he studied her, catching the light along his jaw and cheek, highlighting the beautiful masculinity of his face. Mina glanced away, irritated that she couldn't hold his gaze without noticing him as a man.

"I'd rather live," she said into the taut silence. "But I have nothing to lose."

"There's always something to lose," he murmured.

He spoke so quietly she wasn't sure he meant for her to hear him, and that drew her gaze back to him. "There are worse things than death," she said.

He snorted, an almost-laugh. "Yes. Yes, there are."

She held his gaze this time, not flinching under the bitterness of his comment. She had more than enough of her own to counter his. What did he have to be bitter over, anyway? That he'd sought power and failed? That he'd aligned himself with the wrong side in a war? She had no sympathy for him or his bitterness.

"You do realize going on this mission will mean facing some of those things that are worse than death?" he said.

Another short nod. "For you as well. Maybe worse for you. The Sorcerers must hate you now as much as we Sinnale do."

He chuckled, though there was no humor in it. "I imagine they do. And yes, if they capture me, I'm in for much worse than a simple death. But they won't spare you, Mina of No Family. Don't pretend they will. You've too much emotion, too much anger and hatred. If I can see it, they will. That kind of emotion, combined with your terror, will feed their blood magic better than simple fear ever could."

"I have no intention of being taken alive by the Sorcerers. We succeed or die."

"You might not have a choice."

It was her turn to consider him more closely when she said, "There's always a choice."

To her surprise, he turned away from her, his mouth

turning down in a very faint frown. So. She'd hit a delicate spot. She put the information away for later use.

"You're not as scrawny as most of the Sinnale women have become," he stated in a blunt change of subject. "You still have meat on your bones. Very nice tits. Makes you more fuckable than the rest of the women here. I imagine the men spend a great deal of effort trying to get into your pants."

This was the kind of behavior she'd expected from him. "They warned me you were charming."

Her response earned her a full-throated, surprisingly deep burst of laughter. The sound was so wonderfully rich and sexy, Mina lost her breath. Her mouth dropped open for an instant before she caught herself and snapped it shut.

When he laughed, when he smiled for real, he moved well past beautiful and into the realms of unreal. She felt stunned by him just then, and for a long moment, couldn't drag her attention from the lush, tempting shape of his mouth.

She blinked and straightened in her seat. Damn the man. Why did she have to react to him this way?

"I have always been charming," he said when his laughter eased. "It's my particular gift."

"Speaking of gifts, elves have magic. What's yours?"

"Why do you need to know?"

"Because we're going into enemy territory together. I need to know what use you'll be, outside of the information you provide."

"And what use will you be in watching my back when you've as much as admitted you'd rather stick a knife in it?"

"I'm not going on this mission to watch your back. I'm going to ensure the List of Names is brought back to the council. But I've been working for the better part of the last year and a half as a spy. I've snuck in and out of the part of the city held by the Sorcerers innumerable times in that period. And I'm still alive."

"Can you fight?"

"If needs be."

"Are you any good at it?"

"I'm still alive."

He tilted his head in acknowledgment of the point. "Weapon of choice?"

"Short swords."

"That gets you in dangerously close to an enemy."

"If I have to pull my swords, the enemy is already too close to avoid."

He leaned forward in his chair, resting his forearms on his thighs, and gave her a thoughtful nod. "You're prepared to fight with me to get the List of Names?"

"I'm prepared to do whatever is necessary to end this war once and for all."

"Do you know why your people want the List?"

"Do you?"

He smiled, a slow and seductive lift of his lips, though she wasn't sure he intended the look to be seductive. "The council had to tell me, or I wouldn't cooperate with their questions."

"Doesn't that go against your bargain with them? The reason you're allowed to live here rather than be executed as a traitor?"

"Maybe. They were too anxious for the information to realize that, though."

She didn't want to admit she didn't have all the details. Not to him. Samuel and Iona Brightarrow had assured her that the List of Names, the list containing all the *real* names of the

Sorcerers, would give them the power they needed to end the war. They hadn't told her how, exactly, but she hadn't pushed for an answer either.

It would have something to do with magic—elf magic. She knew enough to realize the real names of a being of power were valuable and dangerous. Most human practitioners like the Sorcerers concealed their real names and instead went by adopted monikers, something that couldn't hold any control over them in a spell.

She also knew why she hadn't been told exactly what magic would be used against the Sorcerers. If she were captured before she could end her life, the less information she had to reveal, the better. As a spy, she'd gotten used to this way of things, because the threat of capture and torture was always a very real possibility.

"They haven't told you, have they?" Althir said after a moment.

She pursed her lips in a scowl and focused on the bars of his cage rather than his face. "They told me everything I needed to know."

He leaned back in his seat again. From the corner of her eye, she could see him studying her.

Finally, he said, "You don't trust me. And you shouldn't. But you'll still travel with me into enemy territory. On the hope that this will end the invasion?"

She nodded.

"Why should I trust you?"

"You shouldn't. But you'll have to rely on me once we cross the border. And you can do that."

"If I betray you?"

"I'll kill you. Happily. That's why I've been allowed to

volunteer for this mission." She finally faced him. "Are you going to betray me?"

He held her gaze for a long moment and then dropped his to stare at the floor. "I don't discuss my magic here. When we get into Noman's Land, I'll tell you what I can do, for my part, beyond provide directions."

He glanced up and caught her unawares, capturing her in a look full of something hot and dangerous. This time, she had no doubt he meant the seduction in his eyes. To her horror, that heat and promise made her pulse jump sharply and her breathing quicken.

"Suffice it to say," he murmured, his tone deep and intimate, "my charm is one of my very useful skills."

She stood so quickly she knocked her chair over. "I doubt the Sorcerers will be bothered with that." She tried to keep her tone hard and impersonal, but even she heard the breathlessness, the hint of a tremor. From his ever-so-slight smirk, she knew he did too. "We leave tomorrow noon. We'll spend the first part of the night in Noman's Land. Then we go in."

He nodded, his expression never changing as he watched her hurry from the basement. Even when she disappeared into the shadows, she felt his gaze hot on her skin.

Once out of the basement, she continued up to the streets and out into the cool night air.

For a long moment, she stood beneath a brightly lit gas lamp, breathing in the faint dampness of approaching rain and letting the chilled breeze cool her overheated skin.

She'd known when stepping forward for this mission that it was going to be the most dangerous thing she'd ever done.

She hadn't realized just how much of that danger would come from the very elf she was partnered with.

Don't miss
DAWN IGNITED
Fire and Tears
Book Three

BOOKS BY ISABO KELLY

Fire and Tears Series

Brightarrow Burning

Darkness Singed

Dawn Ignited

Fire and Tears: Series Collection Books 1-3

Fate's Hand Series

Thief's Desire

Destiny's Seduction

New York Empires Anthologies

Going All In

Icing The Puck

Roughing It

Kellyn's Sacrifice

The Last Guardian

Bonfire Night

ABOUT THE AUTHOR

Isabo Kelly is the award-winning author of numerous science fiction, fantasy, and paranormal romances. She also writes best-selling paranormal romance under the name Kat Simons. Her life has taken her from Las Vegas to Hawaii, where she got her BA in Zoology, back to Vegas where she looked after sharks, then on to Germany and Ireland where she got her Ph.D. in Animal Behavior. Now Isabo focuses on writing. She lives in New York with her beloved family and a library's worth of books.

For more on Isabo, be sure to visit her website or you can find her on social media. She loves hearing from readers!

For more on Isabo and her books

Website: https://www.isabokelly.com
Instagram: https://www.instagram.com/isabokelly/
Threads: https://www.threads.net/@isabokelly

KatSimonsBooks Store
https://www.tanddpublishingbookstore.com

KATSIMONSBOOKS

WELCOMES

ISABO KELLY

Look out for all of Isabo's books as they make their way to her alter ego's store where readers can buy direct from the author, get cool new merch, special editions, and more! Be sure to check out all Isabo's fiction at KatSimonsBooks

https://www.KatSimonsBooks.com